NICE KNIGHT FOR MURDER

NICE KNIGHT FOR MURDER

Philip Daniels

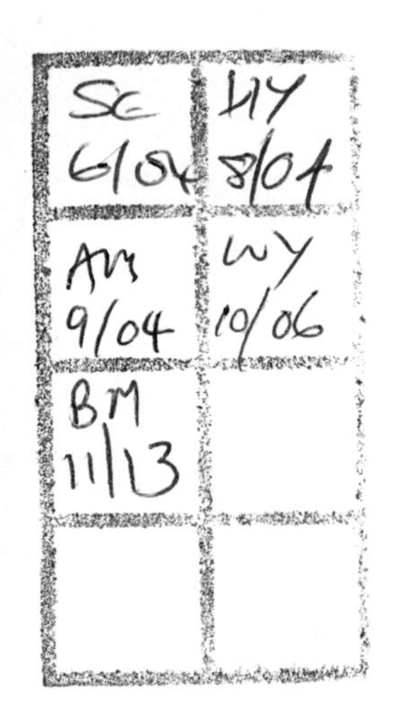

Chivers Press
Bath, England
•
G.K. Hall & Co.
Waterville, Maine USA

This Large Print edition is published by Chivers Press, England, and by G.K. Hall & Co., USA.

Published in 2001 in the U.K. by arrangement with Robert Hale Limited.

Published in 2001 in the U.S. by arrangement with Peter Chambers.

U.K. Hardcover ISBN 0-7540-4566-8 (Chivers Large Print)
U.K. Softcover ISBN 0-7540-4567-6 (Camden Large Print)
U.S. Softcover ISBN 0-7838-9486-4 (Nightingale Series Edition)

The text of this Large Print edition is unabridged.
Other aspects of the book may vary from the original edition.

Set in 16 pt. New Times Roman.

Printed in Great Britain on acid-free paper.

British Library Cataloguing in Publication Data available

Library of Congress Cataloging-in-Publication Data

Daniels, Philip.
Nice knight for murder / by Philip Daniels.
p. cm.
ISBN 0-7838-9486-4 (lg. print : sc : alk. paper)
1. Government investigators—Great Britain—Fiction.
2. Large type books. I. Title.
PR6054.A522 N48 2001
823'.914—dc21 2001024382

CHAPTER ONE

'is due to arrive in Washington tomorrow, for talks with the President.'

The newsreader paused, and when he next spoke his tone had changed to one of hushed reverence.

'We have just heard of the death, at his home in Surrey, of Sir Francis Waterman, the Labour leader. He was sixty-one. More details are coming in, and I will read them at the end of this bulletin.

'The Russians have released preliminary details of the next phase of their space programme—'

* * *

A woman stared in disbelief at the television screen. Dead? He did say dead, didn't he? Must be a mistake.

No, they didn't make mistakes about things like that. Dead? Not Frank. Yes. Frank was dead. She shook her head, and rose slowly to her feet. They'd be here soon, she was under no illusion about that. She had to get away somewhere. Anywhere. Pain racked at her chest, and large tears formed in her eyes. No. She shook her head impatiently. Not now. She wouldn't let herself give in now. Time for that later, when she was safely away and alone. Alone. Oh, she was alone all right. She'd be alone from now on, and she had better get used to the idea. Somehow, she guided unwilling feet into the bedroom. There, she reached above the wardrobe and lifted down a green soft leather case. Placing it on the bed she snapped the catches and opened the lid. Shoes. She'd start with the shoes.

* * *

In a public house in London's East End a group of men sat, watching the news bulletin.

'D'you hear that?' said one. 'Frank Waterman. Who'd have thought it? He always looks so well. You knew him, didn't you, Tom?'

Tom Pardoe nodded. His face was grave as he replied.

'Yes, I knew him. I tell you this, that man can't be replaced. The working people of this country will never know what he's done for them. This is a bad day for the working man.'

One of the others coughed.

'I'spect you're right, Tom,' he said carefully. 'Still, he done all right for himself, didn't he? I mean, he got sirred and that.'

Pardoe looked at him sourly.

'You think that meant anything, to a man like him. Eighteen hours a day he worked. Saturdays, Sundays, even Christmas if he had to. While all his lovely members were snivelling about a thirty-five-hour week, Frank Waterman was working over a hundred. Fancy your chances, killing yourself like that, do you? Think it's all right, so long as somebody calls you 'sir'?'

Tom Pardoe's voice was rising, and there was tension in the group. One of the older men said gently,

'Now, now, Tommy, you're not the only one who feels things. I met Frank meself, years ago now, but I've always liked him. I think what we should all do is to get a drink in, and have a proper toast to his memory. Bit of respect, that's what I think.'

Some of the anger went from Pardoe's face.

'You're right there, Cyril. And it's my shout. What's everybody going to have?'

*   *   *

In a quiet street in South London, a young man pushed open the kitchen door. His mother was busy ironing his football jersey for the game on Saturday. She smiled at him.

'Got fed up with the news, have you? All them bombings and terrorists and that. Can't think why you bother with it. Upsets me, it does. What have they done now? Blown up the Kremlin?'

Her son looked at the calm smiling face and wished there were some way to avoid the next few minutes.

'Mum, I want you to leave that for a minute. Come and sit down. There's something I want to tell you.'

'Leave it?' she echoed. 'I'm nearly finished. I'll come in a minute.'

'Now, Mum,' he said urgently. 'Please.'

Mystified, she turned and switched off the iron. His face was very serious, and it set her mind racing. He'd got some girl into trouble, that's what it was. Couldn't be his job, they'd been laughing about that over tea. No. It was a girl, that's what it was. Well, if some little chippie thought she was going to get her son that way, we'd see about that.

He took her by the hand and led her through into the living-room where the news was still in progress.

'Better switch that thing off, if we're going to talk,' she suggested.

'No, Mum. I want you to see it.'

The young man swallowed. The news was getting near the end. If he didn't tell her now, she'd hear it from a stranger.

'It's about Uncle Frank, Ma,' he forced out the words. 'There's some bad news.'

A hand flew to her breast, and there was alarm in her eyes.

'Frank? He's not ill, is he? He works too hard. I'm always on at him. How many times have you heard me—'

'It's not that. It's real bad news, Mum.

Uncle Frank is—well, Uncle Frank's dead.'

'No.'

She said it quite decisively, her face resolute. Frank was not dead. He wouldn't die just like that. Not a man like Frank. It was out of the question. He was too important. Important people didn't just die. There'd be plenty of notice. There'd be doctors and days of anxiety, and all that. Time for people to get used to the idea.

The boy stared unhappily at her grim face. Well, he'd done his best. The newsreader would have to tell her after all.

'And now, finally, here is the latest information we have about the death today of Sir Francis Waterman.'

* * *

The saloon bar was at its noisy usual when the messenger from *The Globe* pushed open the door and began to look round. The man he was seeking was hunched at the far end of the bar, deep in conversation with a celebrated cartoonist.

'Ah, there you are, Mr Law,' began the newcomer.

Cavendish Law, known throughout the political world as The Claw, turned sleepy eyes on the intruder.

'Ah yourself, o harbinger of doom. Don't tell me, the cookery woman's on heat again, and

I've got to write tomorrow's menu.'

The messenger grinned.

'I think you'd better come, Mr Law. It's big, he says.'

'Big is it? What a boastful fellow our editor is. Is it him the cookery woman's chasing, then?'

The cartoonist raised a hand, almost losing his balance in the process.

'Might make a nice little picture,' he drawled.

Law sniffed.

'You haven't seen Madame Chef. She used to be the bearded lady until the circus left town. Has to shave three times a day.' Turning to the hapless visitor, he smiled kindly. 'Don't look so worried, laddie. Plonk the rear section on this handsome padded stool and observe a great newspaperman at work. If you care to supply a small libation I will advise you on the intricacies of a journalistic career.'

Some career, thought the messenger bitterly. All he seemed to have achieved hitherto was a name as a maker of coffee, and a certain skill in locating missing reporters. The editor had warned him there might be a problem with The Claw. He had also warned him that the reason for the recall was not for broadcasting. As a precaution, he had scribbled a short note on a piece of paper, and this he now held up, so that only Law could see the message. It read, simply, 'Frank

Waterman is dead.'

Law blinked at it, then frowned.

'You're not a joking type, sonny, I trust?'

'No jokes, Mr Law.'

Slowly, the columnist raised his glass, saluted the ceiling, and drained it.

'So, the bastard's gone at last. There is still some justice in this wicked world. I shall come on the inst.'

His drinking companion squinted suspiciously.

'Something on?' he demanded.

Law eased himself upright, keeping his weight on his hands until he was safely balanced.

'Nothing for you, old man,' he denied. 'The office cat's gone up the chimney again. He won't come down for anyone but me. Might see you later. Lead on, my son. We'll pick up some flea powder on the way.'

The cartoonist heaved his shoulders.

'Lying sod,' he grumbled.

* * *

'Finally, gentlemen, I would say this. The fact that we are all here tonight, enjoying this hospitality in such a convivial atmosphere, is in itself an indication of the progress we have all made in our efforts for clearer understanding and mutual goodwill. Two years ago, you would not have invited me here. Even if you had, I should have refused. That is now behind us. Tonight, I am very pleased to have been asked, and even more pleased with the circumstances which have brought us together. I do not pretend that all our difficulties have been resolved. There is much yet to be done. But I regard this as a milestone, gentlemen. A milestone on the road to a better future. For your people, for my people, and for this great country of ours. Thank you.'

There was enthusiastic applause all round the vast banqueting-suite as George Watling sat down. Two places away, the chairman rose to thank him and bring the formal proceedings to a close. The brandy was circulating now, and Watling was glad of the opportunity to refuse. It always made him feel that he had scored a point when he declined a drink. It put him one up on these soft-living people, or so he fondly imagined. A waiter leaned deferentially at his side, with a whispered message.

'There's a telephone call for you, Mr Watling.'

The great man frowned.

'Not now,' he said testily. 'Tell them to try again in an hour.'

'I took the liberty of suggesting that it wasn't a very good time, sir, but I was told the matter is very urgent. It's your London office. They're very persistent.'

'Headquarters?' returned Watling, obviously

puzzled. 'At this hour?'

What the devil could it be, he wondered? There was nothing on down there at that particular moment. Something disastrous must have happened for them to be calling him at nine o'clock at night.

'All right, I'll be along.'

Turning to his neighbour, he explained the situation and apologised, before getting up and making his exit. Two hundred pairs of eyes watched him speculatively as he headed for the door. It couldn't be one of his famous acts of rudeness, not after the speech he'd just made. Something must be up.

The telephone was in the manager's private office. Watling waited until the waiter had closed the door behind him, then said,

'This is George Watling. What's up now?'

'George, are you alone?'

It was Len Bowan's voice. It would have to be something important for the General Secretary to be calling at this time of night.

'It's all right Len, I'm on my own. You sound nervous.'

Without preamble the voice at the other end announced, 'It's Frank. He died a few minutes ago.'

Watling stared at the receiver in his hand, disbelieving.

'Frank?' he repeated. 'Bloody hell. What happened?'

'Don't know the details yet. The point is,

George, you'll have to come to London. I've got the General Purposes Committee tomorrow, and I can't hold those bastards by myself. It wouldn't have mattered so much if Frank had been coming. As it is, I'm going to need you.'

'Hold on, Len. I'm in the middle of these talks. I can't just walk out, not when we're doing so well.'

Len Bowman's tone became firmer.

'I'm sorry George. I wouldn't ask it if it wasn't urgent. Billy's up there with you. He'll have to do the best he can. The meeting is in this building at two-thirty.'

'Thanks very much,' said Watling sourly. 'You're not giving me much choice, are you?'

'You can hardly blame me because Frank died on us,' retorted Bowman. 'There's going to have to be a lot of rethinking in the next few days.'

That was true enough, reflected the listening man. Frank Waterman's death was going to upset all sorts of things. It was also, as he was very quick to recognise, going to provide many opportunities for people to advance in various directions.

'Don't worry, Len, I'll be there,' he said firmly. 'If these bloody splinter groups think they can take advantage of Frank's absence, they've got another think coming. Tell you what, I could get to your office by one-thirty, straight from the airport. We can have a sandwich, and you can bring me up to date before we go in. That suit you?'

Bowman's voice was tinged with relief when he replied.

'That'll be fine, George. See you tomorrow then. Half-past one.'

Watling's face was thoughtful as he replaced the receiver. Frank Waterman dead. Well, well, well. Funny how we can never really be sure of our reactions. Here was a man he'd hated for thirty years, and now he was gone. If anyone had asked him a few minutes earlier, he would have said it would be a damned good thing when the world was finally rid of Sir Francis Waterman.

Now that it was a fact, he found the news gave him no pleasure at all. Not even a sense of satisfaction.

Strange.

* * *

'The point is, Alan, Guest Appearance is scheduled for eight-thirty, and Sir Francis is the main attraction. The nine o'clock news follows, and there'll be all kinds of follow-up stories about the man's death. It's not only incongruous, it's ghoulish.'

Alan Player fiddled with his cigarette lighter. He understood the problem perfectly well without Peter harping on it all the time. The responsibility for programme scheduling was his, and the decision would have to be his. But, as he knew from bitter experience, there was no right or wrong in situations like these. Whatever decision he came to could later prove to be hopelessly wrong, not because of the conditions which applied at the time it was made, but because of subsequent events which no one could possibly foresee.

'Except a bloody soothsayer,' he said aloud, without fully intending to.

'Eh? Sorry?'

Peter Davis looked at him anxiously. He hoped Alan wasn't beginning to crack up. Six years was a big stint in his exacting job, far longer than anyone had previously managed to hold it down.

Player picked up the telephone and dialled. He had decided on a most unusual course.

'Hallo, Mike,' he said carefully. 'Alan Player. Would you be good enough to ask if His Lordship could spare me a minute? Yes, I know, but this is a bit out of the ordinary run. Call me back, will you?'

He leaned back, and expelled a long sighing breath.

This, he reflected, is only the beginning of it.

CHAPTER TWO

Detective Chief Superintendent Wilfred Hampton yawned and stretched his arms. It was ten forty-five, and he'd have to make up his mind. There was a film starting at ten-fifty, which looked as if it might be interesting. The problem was, once he started to watch it he knew he'd stay with it to the end, and that would mean he wouldn't get to bed until a quarter to one in the morning.

The next day was going to be a busy one, and he ought to be getting a good night's sleep. That was the trouble with living by yourself. There wasn't anyone to care about what you did. Funny the way life evolves. Three years ago the house had always seemed to be full of people. Both his sons were still at home then, and quite often there would be friends of theirs, staying the night, or days on end sometimes. And of course there had been Molly, always quietly cheerful, keeping the whole mechanism ticking over. He tried to avoid thinking about Molly as much as he could in a house filled with her memory.

It was all so different now. The boys gone out into the world, as boys have to, and Molly—Molly was dead, he reminded himself firmly. She had been gone for almost two years now, and it was high time he adjusted to his new position.

Ten forty-seven.

If he didn't get up from his chair in the next three minutes the film would start, and the decision would be taken from him.

The doorbell chimed. He'd have to get up now. Climbing reluctantly to his feet, he began to cross towards the door, changed his mind, and went first to the television set, switching it off. That resolved one problem. Now he could give his attention to getting rid of the caller and still get to bed at a reasonable time.

There was a man standing under the porch light. Tallish man, well-dressed, about thirty-five years old. Face was vaguely familiar.

'Good evening,' said Hampton.

'You may remember me, Mr Hampton. I'm Doctor Mellows, Lawrence Mellows. I was in attendance when one of your constables was shot in that bank raid at Guildford last year.'

Mellows. Oh yes, he had him now. Good chap. Methodical, he recalled.

'Yes, of course, Doctor. Come in, won't you. Place is a bit of a mess I'm afraid. I only tidy up at weekends.'

He led the way through into the living-room. Lawrence Mellows followed him, with practised eyes picking up the certain indications of a house occupied by a solitary man.

'Can I get you something, a drink? Should be some Scotch around somewhere.'

'No thank you,' Mellows refused. 'I had some beer not long ago, and I don't take chances when I'm driving.'

Wilf Hampton nodded impassively. Funny how many people said that in his hearing these days, or something like it. He couldn't see why they bothered. Anybody would think he went around with a supply of breathalyser bags in his pocket.

'Very well,' he replied. 'Well then, Doctor?'

Mellows' face was serious now.

'Yes,' he said quietly. 'I don't know whether I'm doing the right thing in coming to you. The fact is, I wanted to talk to the most senior police officer I could think of, and since we had met over that bank business, I decided to talk to you.'

'Ah.'

Hampton nodded encouragingly, wondering at the same time what guilty secret his visitor wanted to get off his chest.

'Did you hear the news about Sir Francis Waterman's death?' The doctor looked at him anxiously.

'I heard it on the nine o'clock news,' confirmed the policeman, somewhat puzzled by the question.

'I was called out for that,' went on Mellows. 'I'm on the emergency rota this week.'

'Really? It must have been quite a surprise to find you had such a well-known patient. Emergency rota, you say? How did that come about, doctor? 999 call, was it?'

'Yes. His housekeeper found him unconscious and called emergency at once.'

'Sensible woman. What was the cause of death, Doctor? They didn't give it on the T.V.'

Mellows' face was worried as he replied.

'That's just it. That's why I'm here. I'm not satisfied that his death was due to natural causes.'

'Not—' Hampton raised his eyebrows. 'Are you saying that Sir Francis may have committed suicide?'

The doctor shrugged.

'I don't know. My preliminary observations suggest the presence of some form of poison. That could mean it was self-administered. Or, on the other hand, it could mean something else.'

Murder. The word formed itself inside the chief superintendent's head, but he didn't want to say it out loud. Not at that moment.

'Well now, this is very interesting, Doctor Mellows. Very interesting indeed. But I don't quite see why you should come to tell me about it. Surely our local people are on the job, aren't they? I'll have somebody over a slow fire if they're not.'

Lawrence Mellows could not suppress a half-smile at this professional reaction.

'They are at the house,' he confirmed. 'There's a sergeant in charge—young man named Austin. I'm sure you would have no complaint against him. A most efficient and courteous man. Knew exactly how to deal with the reporters. I was thankful he was there.'

Austin. Yes. Fat chap, with fair hair. Yes, he'd be a good choice for a job like this.

'Was it Sergeant Austin's idea that you should approach me?' asked the chief superintendent casually.

Better not have been. If it was, there'd be a certain P.C. Austin on traffic duty quite shortly. The import of the question was not lost on Mellows.

'No. I have told the sergeant nothing. He regards his presence at the house as coming under the heading of protection of private grief. I think that was the phrase he used. Anyway, he's doing it very well. Coming here was entirely my own idea.'

Hampton looked at him narrowly.

'Doctor Mellows, I think we are going to have to regard this as an official visit, from this point onwards. I suggest we'd both be more comfortable if we sat down.'

The visitor nodded thoughtfully. Official visit. Good. For the past two hours his mind had been in a turmoil of uncertainty, almost from the moment he detected those tell-tale symptoms in the dead man. His instant reaction had been to pass the information to the nearest policeman and let subsequent events take their course. Then, as the wider implications of the affair began to dawn on him, he had restrained himself. Now, he would be able to explain his reasons to this highly experienced man, and with any luck at all his decision would be justified.

When they were both settled, Wilf Hampton picked up his pipe and began to press tobacco into the bowl.

'Doctor Mellows, would you be good enough to start at the beginning? I mean, from the moment you arrived at the house?'

Lawrence Mellows cleared his throat.

'Certainly. I found Sir Francis, seated in a—'

'Whoa,' Hampton interrupted. 'You're going too fast, Doctor. First of all, you knocked at the door, I imagine? Start from there, please.'

'Ah yes. I see. No. I didn't have to knock. This lady, Mrs Cooper, was standing outside waiting for me. The door was wide open.'

'Mrs Cooper?' repeated Hampton. 'That the housekeeper?'

'Yes. She said "Thank God you're here, Doctor," or something like that, and took me inside.'

'Did you see anyone else in the house?'

'No. And Mrs Cooper told me later there was no one else there but Sir Francis and herself.'

'All right. So she took you into this room. What sort of room was it?'

'It was Sir Francis' study. Place where he did a lot of his work. More or less what you'd expect. A desk, a typewriter, couple of chairs. Books everywhere, naturally.'

'And I think you found him in one of the chairs. Was that a working sort of chair, or an armchair, or what?'

'It was a heavy leather chair, with arms. Not the kind you could sit in if you were writing. On the other hand, reading is part of work, and no doubt Sir Francis had to read a great deal to keep up with what's going on. You'll be familiar with that one, as we all are.'

Hampton nodded, in grim agreement. One of his chief complaints was about the quantity of reading-matter he had to absorb.

'Only too familiar, Doctor. Now then, the dead man was sitting in this chair. How was he dressed? I mean, was he dressed for the street, or was he ready for bed, or what?'

'Neither, really. He was just in casual clothes. Soft shirt, cardigan, pair of slacks. In fact, much as you are at this moment. Evening at home sort of clothes, I suppose one could say.'

The policeman grunted, not liking the comparison too well.

'What time exactly was this when you first saw the dead man?'

'Eight-fourteen. I noted the time most carefully.'

'Good. Were you able to make any estimation of how long he had been dead?'

Mellows nodded.

'Yes. As a matter of fact, I can be rather more precise about that than one usually can. Sir Francis must have died somewhere between seven p.m. and eight-fourteen.'

The chief superintendent looked at him quizzically.

'Very precise indeed, doctor,' he complimented. 'Our medical evidence is not always so exact.'

Despite the apparent tribute, Mellows was conscious that he was being pressed for more detail.

'Yes, I understand what you mean,' he concurred, 'but that is not entirely medical evidence. Sir Francis had an early dinner, six-thirty in fact. It was only a scratch meal, as I gather from Mrs Cooper. That didn't take him very long, and afterwards he took his coffee into the study, to work. At seven o'clock the housekeeper went in to ask if he wanted more coffee, but he said he hadn't quite finished. Then—'

'Just a moment,' interrupted his listener. 'Did he seem all right at that moment?'

'Yes. A bit short-tempered, but Mrs Cooper seems to be quite used to that.'

'M'm. And she was quite clear about the time? That's odd, wouldn't you say?'

'Normally, yes. But her favourite television programme was due to start at seven-fifteen. She was anxious not to be interrupted, once it started. That's why she went back again ten minutes later. Sir Francis seemed to be unconscious, and she couldn't rouse him. She thought he must have had a heart-attack or something, and dialled 999 at once.'

Chief Superintendent Hampton beamed with approval. The more he heard about Mrs Cooper, the more he warmed to her. She was going to make a valuable witness, by the sound of her.

'That would have been about ten past seven, then,' he muttered. 'What makes you place the time of death as late as eight-fourteen?'

The doctor looked at him in surprise.

'Because that was the time when I examined him. He was certainly dead then, as I am qualified to say. Until that moment he could have been in a deep coma, close to death certainly, but not necessarily dead. Mrs Cooper may have thought he was, but that is not medical evidence, as you and I well know.'

Wilf Hampton smiled inwardly, realising that he was in danger of treading on professional corns.

'Quite understand, Doctor,' he soothed. 'So, you were satisfied that your patient was dead. Please tell me what you did next.'

Mellows nodded, mollified.

'I didn't like the look of things. Certainly, there had been no cardiac eruption, and there was evidence that death had been caused as the result of some poisonous substance. This is just on a superficial examination, you understand. I should require in-depth tests to be positive as to the origin of those indications. That was when I summoned the police. As soon as I explained the name, they responded at once.'

'And did you say anything about your suspicions?' pressed Hampton.

'No. No, I didn't. I simply said that some kind of police presence would be necessary at once, because of the prominence of Sir Francis. Obviously, the reporters would soon get wind of his death, and it was essential that the proper authorities should be present. Oh, you need have no concern, Mr Hampton. Your local people knew exactly what to do.'

Good for them, reflected Hampton. Lucky for them, too. But he had yet to ask the sixty-four thousand dollar question.

'I'm glad to hear it,' he responded. 'But now, Doctor, I should very much like to know what made you decide to keep this information to yourself.'

Mellows sat back in his chair, hands pressed together in his best consulting-room manner.

'But I have not kept it to myself,' he contradicted. 'I have repeated it at the earliest opportunity. At an appropriate level. Your level. Shall I go on?'

The veteran policeman nodded his head.

'Yes, Doctor. I think you'd better.'

The visitor produced a packet of cigarettes and lit one. His host could scarcely object, with the pipe pulling nicely and the atmosphere already beginning to cloud.

'We are speaking of Sir Francis Waterman. No ordinary man, Sir Francis, as we both know well. His death is going to cause quite a stir in many quarters. In high places, and in private places. Prominent trade union leader, one-time Cabinet minister, race-equality champion. Also, in the past few years, a regular broadcaster and television personality, very popular with the general public. There is also the private side of his life, which has been less private lately. I am sure that only the goodwill of the Press has damped down quite a lot of publicity in that direction. A very public man, Sir Francis, and a very private man too. I have no idea, naturally, of who might want him dead. Frankly, that is of no concern to me. What I am concerned about is that the nature of his passing should not be made public, until such time as people in authority have been able to assess the position.'

His host stared at him wide-eyed.

'A cover-up?' he said in disbelief. 'Are you suggesting some kind of a cover-up, Doctor?'

Lawrence Mellows smiled.

'I suggest nothing. Let me explain my position in this. I am a man with certain ambitions, Mr Hampton. I have no intention of settling down as a country G.P. for the rest of my life. I am active in a number of directions, and beginning to become known.

My future, until a couple of hours ago, was set fair. Once I realised that there could be sinister implications in Waterman's death, I realised at the same time that I had a responsibility. I could at once inform your sergeant, and let the normal machinery roll into action. That would have made the matter public property in a matter of hours. The result could be that every news agency in the country would be howling for blood, poking their noses into every conceivable aspect of Waterman's life, causing God knows what kind of disruption in places that I can only guess at. And who would be responsible for this chaos? Lawrence Mellows, M.D. Some bumbling general practitioner who, at one stroke, managed to make enemies in every high office in the land. Now, do you understand?'

The policeman sucked deeply on his pipe. He understood all right. This bloody man was keeping his nose clean by the simple expedient of handing over the problem to one Detective Chief Superintendent Hampton.

'Does anyone know you're here?' he demanded.

'No. I am simply out on routine duties, so far as everyone is concerned.'

'H'm.' Hampton went to the fireplace, knocking out his pipe into the remnants of the fire. 'Well, Doctor, I'm not going to pretend to be very pleased with you. Frankly, I wish I'd never laid eyes on you. Either that, or that I'd gone fishing this week. Still, that's as may be. You're here, and I seem to be stuck with this. But your part is not finished, not by a long shot. There will be people wanting to talk to you. I don't think you'll be getting home just yet.'

Mellows nodded.

'I rather expected that. I have some pyjamas and a toothbrush in the car.'

Despite his annoyance, Hampton could not suppress a grin.

'First thing we must do is to get the inquest delayed. I imagine your coroner's people are pretty busy, aren't they?'

'Snowed under, I believe. Some problem with a go-slow on the paper-work.'

'First class. We must make sure we don't do anything to hurry them up. And now, I'm going to do something only a very brave copper would do.'

There was a reluctant twinkle in his eye as he waited for the invited question. 'What might that be, Mr Hampton?' Hampton rolled his eyes. 'I'm going to get the Chief Constable out of bed.'

CHAPTER THREE

David Oliver Nicholas Bradman stifled a yawn and flexed his muscles as best he could in a sitting position. He'd been perched on a hard wooden chair in the cheerless little anteroom for over thirty minutes and was beginning to wonder if they'd forgotten about him. Whoever 'they' might be. All he knew was that he'd been withdrawn without ceremony from a very promising investigation and told to report to this ramshackle place in South London. The seniority of the man who gave the instruction had left him no room even for a token protest.

A man less familiar with the odd workings of certain sections of the Department might have been forgiven for thinking there had been some mistake. The address proved to be that of a side-street newsagent and tobacconist. There was one customer in the shop, a woman, who was avidly reading her way through a paperback novel, protected from the shopkeeper's inspection by a revolving book-rack. When the newcomer entered, she replaced it quickly and became absorbed in reading the other titles on display.

'Yes?'

The man behind the counter was fifty years old, and resigned to a life of preventing small children from rifling his wrapped-sweet counter.

'V.A.T.' announced Bradman. 'Half-yearly inspection. They told you I was coming, didn't they?'

The other man nodded.

'Go through, will you? The books are ready. My wife will make you a nice cup of tea. Ask her to bring me one out, would you?'

He raised a flap in the counter and motioned Bradman through, and out into a narrow passageway leading from the shop. Behind him he could hear the shopkeeper grumbling about invasion of privacy and government snoopers.

'From the V.A.T., is it?'

The question came from a woman who could only be the soulmate of the seedy shopkeeper. In the poor light it wasn't possible to be accurate as to the number of cardigans she was wearing, but Bradman got to three before abandoning the project.

'Yes,' he nodded. 'Your husband asked whether you'd be kind enough to take him a cup of tea.'

'Him and his tea,' she sniffed. 'Fourth cup this morning, that'll be. Ought to run a tea-shop, not a sweet-shop. Would you go upstairs, please? All the paper work's up there.'

He went up the bare, protesting stairway, glad of the support provided by a rickety banister.

'This way.'

A man stood at an open door, beckoning to him. The newcomer followed him into a small room, which smelled of damp. There was one wooden chair, placed close to a second door.

'Sit down there, please. Shouldn't be long.'

The man went away, and he parked himself dutifully, wondering about the house, and what other uses were made of it. He knew better than to ask questions, but there were no rules against speculation. A man had to do something to pass the time. Already, half an hour had been frittered away.

The door near him opened.

'Come in, please.'

He went through and found himself in a much larger room. Behind a long wooden table sat three men.

'Morning, Bradman, take a seat.'

The chair facing the table was twin to the one he'd just vacated, but he wasn't concerned with the chair. He was too intent on the three celebrated faces now looking at him. Strange bedfellows, he was thinking.

On the left was Charlie Bolt, the pugnacious leader of the TUC middle-of-the-road faction. The man on the right was Hugh Robertson, Government spokesman on Internal Affairs. Opposite Bradman, and seated between their two very different viewpoints, was the inperturbable face of Sir Edward Houston, reputed to be the ultimate head of Bradman's own department. No one was certain, and as with everything else, no one ever asked.

It was Sir Edward who spoke first.

'Well now, Bradman, we'll not bother with introductions. You know who these gentlemen are, so there is no need for me to stress the importance of this interview. The point is, they don't know who you are. There is a job of work to be done. I am confident you are the right man for it, but that is really beside the point. These gentlemen have to satisfy themselves with my recommendation, and that is why you are here. You understand?'

'Yes, sir.'

Sir Edward nodded, and turned towards Charlie Bolt.

'Would you like to lead us off, Charlie?'

'I would.' Bolt looked at the candidate shrewdly. 'What are we going to call you?'

Bradman was puzzled.

'Sir.'

'Your name, man.'

'Oh. David, sir.'

The wise face nodded.

'I can read what's in front of me, thanks. It's your initials I'm thinking of. D.O.N., and your name's Bradman. Father a cricket fan, was he?'

'Yes. He wanted to call me Donald, but my mother wouldn't have it. He got round the problem by thinking of my initials.'

The trade union leader nodded.

'But you don't play cricket I see. Bit of a

boxer instead. Why's that?'

Strange questions, these, reflected Bradman.

'First of all, I'm not very good at cricket. It's too slow to suit me. With boxing, you can get in the ring and have your go, then it's over.'

Bolt smiled encouragingly.

'More your style, is it? Don't like a lot of hanging about. Prefer to rush in, and get things sorted out?'

Cunning old sod, trying to trick a man that way.

'By no means, sir,' rebutted the younger man. 'We were talking about how I spend my leisure-time. There isn't very much of it, and I have to get results quickly. Most of my work is quite different. Methodical, painstaking, never any hurried decisions. If I make a wrong move when I'm boxing, all that happens is that I suffer for it. A wrong decision in my working life can have far more serious results. That's why I don't make any.'

Was he hitting the right note, he wondered? It was all very well to sound confident, but that last contribution could be interpreted as coming from a swelled head. Ah well, it was said now.

His interrogator turned to the chairman.

'That'll do me for a minute, Sir Edward.'

'Thank you, Charlie. Hugh?'

The Government man smiled, and looked at Bradman.

'According to the information I have, there

doesn't seem to be any young woman in your life. At twenty-six I find that a bit unusual.'

They didn't think he was gay, surely?

'There was a girl, sir. We were to have been married, but she was killed in a plane crash two years ago. I haven't quite recovered from that yet.'

Evidently they hadn't found out about Veronica, which was a relief. If these people had any indication that he was having an affair with the wife of one of the country's top industrialists, he would be leaving in two parts. His body would exit through the door, and his career via the window.

Hugh Robertson asked one or two further questions, the relevance of which passed him by, then the interview reached an abrupt end. Before he quite realised it, Sir Edward was saying,

'Just wait outside, will you? I'll call you again before too long.'

It was back to the other hard chair, but this time he had a lot to think about. What kind of a job had they in mind for him, these ill-assorted people? It had to be something really weird to get Charlie Bolt and Hugh Robertson sitting at the same table. They were always sniping at each other, in the newspapers and on public platforms, all over the place. Some strange ideas of interview techniques, too. All they seemed to learn was that he was a non-homosexual boxer, whatever they might deduce from that.

He waited a very long time before the door of the interview-room opened again. Sir Edward stood there, beckoning him inside. The others had gone, and he realised that the curtains at one side of the room must cover not a window, as he had first supposed, but another door.

When they were both seated, Sir Edward smiled thinly.

'Good. They like you.'

'But they didn't ask me anything, sir. Nothing relevant. Nothing about what I do know, or what have I done.'

'Of course not,' was the rejoinder. 'Technical details of that kind don't concern those people. They leave all that to me, take it for granted. They knew that if you weren't up to the job I wouldn't waste their time by bringing them here.'

Bradman was still puzzled.

'In that case, sir, why didn't they just leave it to you?'

Sir Edward shook his head.

'Because they are involved. Heavily involved. They wouldn't just take my word. They both might have to answer for the outcome of this—um—undertaking, and they won't be put in the position of having to say they left it all to somebody else. No, they had to see you, satisfy themselves. Cut of your jib, and all that. Anyway, you've passed.'

There was a certain dry satisfaction in his tone, and Bradman knew that he had scored a small victory, which would be duly marked down in some mysterious archive, which he would never see.

'As of this moment, Bradman, you are relieved of all and any other responsibilities. Your social life is also at an end until the job is done. Can't stop you sleeping, of course, but I hope there won't be too much even of that. Time is of the essence.'

Since there was no trace of lightness either in the tone or in the speaker's face, Bradman realised the sleep reference was not a joke. He waited impatiently for details of the assignment.

'We are concerned about the death of Sir Francis Waterman. The body was first examined by a local G.P. Luckily for us, this chap has his wits about him, and he is also ambitious. Name of Mellows, Doctor Lawrence Mellows. No, you needn't bother to take notes. I'll pass this stuff to you before you leave.'

Bradman slid the silver pencil back into his inside pocket, and waited.

'Doctor Mellows suspected, and it has subsequently been confirmed, that Sir Francis did not die a natural death. He was poisoned. Your job is to find out who did it, and why.'

Poisoned? A murder case? This was not his bag at all.

'With respect, sir, surely the police are much better qualified, much better equipped, and so forth?'

He would have gone on, but for the raised hand on the other side of the desk.

'You are absolutely right. The police would do the job far better, but unfortunately we cannot avail ourselves of their services. Too many people would be involved. This is a very private matter. The total number of people we can afford to have privy to all the facts is one. You are that one.'

Thanks very much, thought Bradman. The implications behind his master's words were not lost on him. At twenty-six, many other young man might well be preening himself at this stage. He had been selected for a task of considerable importance and delicacy, and that was a flattering reflection of the esteem in which he was held by people in high places. Any man, but especially one as young as Bradman, might well be forgiven at least some feeling of self-satisfaction.

But Bradman was not an ordinary man. He had already spent several years in a curious twilit world, where substance was frequently shadow, and the seemingly commonplace often grotesque. A world where rewards were negligible, and penalties severe. He had no illusions about this new situation. The bookmakers had a useful phrase to describe it. He was on a hiding to nothing. Success in the venture would bring him no more than a grunt from the other end of a telephone. Failure could easily mean the end of his career. He'd been around long enough to know one thing clearly. His people were not concerned about the details of failure, only in failure itself. And there was no room in the organisation for people who failed.

'I'll have to talk to a lot of people, sir,' he pointed out. 'What is to be my cover?'

Sir Edward eyed him carefully. Promising chap, this. It was in some ways a pity that he should have to be put to quite such a test this early in his career. Still, there was no help for it. An older man would run too much risk of exciting interest in certain quarters. This one was about the right age, and appearance, to be accepted as a not-very-important official, tying up loose ends for procedural purposes.

'Before we get to the finer points of detail,' he said drily, 'let me explain more about the job itself. Sir Francis, as you must know, was a man of many parts. At an age where many people are either retired, or contemplating retirement, he has been in the forefront of numerous issues, political and otherwise. A man of quite extraordinary vigour, and a man who got things done. He was also a man who refused to toe the line if he felt that a policy was basically wrong. That particular facet of his make-up was the only thing that kept him from the tenancy of Number Ten.'

In departmental parlance, the reference meant that Sir Francis Waterman, if he had not been something of an enfant terrible, would have been Prime Minister. Bradman nodded, to indicate that he understood, but refrained from interrupting.

Sir Edward resumed.

'Naturally, the public loved him. They always like to see someone in authority who questions the status quo. He was a good-looking man, with a great air of authority, and a wicked sense of humour. He's been using this television programme—the name escapes me—'

'—Guest Appearance, sir,' contributed Bradman.

'Ah yes, just so.' Sir Edward gave one of his thin smiles in acknowledgement. The name of the programme was on the desk in front of him, but he wanted to ascertain whether this young man kept abreast of such matters. Too many people in the department became so immersed in the shadowy non-world they inhabited that they tended to lose touch with the commonplace. It would happen to Bradman in time, but that time was not yet. Good. Another point in his favour. 'As I was going to say, Sir Francis has been making use of this television thing to further his image with the public, and doing it very well I am told. The television people have a points system of some kind, to assess the popularity of programmes, and Guest Appearance has been climbing steadily ever since Sir Francis first took part. So, to sum up. Here we have a man who is a thorn in the side of his own party, and one with ready access to the nation at large, who think it is from him that the sunshine originates.'

That was the nearest Sir Edward Houston had ever come to making a joke in Bradman's hearing. Some response was called for, and so he produced his best imitation of the master's own, thin smile.

'Despite the opinion of the public, there are many people who consider Sir Francis a dangerous man. This is particularly true of some of the more extreme organisations, and I think you will know the people I am speaking of. There are many who will have heard of his death with relief, if not positive satisfaction. It is not impossible that some hothead from among their ranks could be the responsible party. You look as though you want to interrupt.'

'If I may, sir. Take your point about some of those weirdos, of course, but I would have looked for some different method from people like that. A good, satisfying piece of violence. Like a car-bomb, or a shotgun, something dramatic. Poison is not usually the weapon of the assassin, sir.'

'I am inclined to agree with you, but nevertheless the possibility is not to be discounted. H'm?'

'No, Sir. Naturally not.'

'As you say, the choice of weapon is unusual. Far more domestic than public, and that brings us to the other part of the investigation. I am speaking of Sir Francis' private life. Is it possible that you have heard anything in that direction?'

Bradman's hesitation was only momentary. This was no time to be pussy-footing around, he decided.

'Well, sir, rumour only, you understand. Quite strong rumour, though. I have heard that Sir Francis may have had certain extra-marital difficulties.'

'Couldn't have phrased it better myself,' conceded Sir Edward. 'Yes, I think that could be said, with safety. The plain fact is, the man couldn't keep his hands off the women. He's been very lucky not to have landed in a courtroom more than once. Now, reverting to your earlier point, you would probably find that a profitable source of enquiry. Women and poison have been associated in all our minds since time began. Yes, that could well be the answer.'

His voice tailed away, as if he had finished speaking. Bradman hoped such was not the case. There was a lot more he needed to know yet.

'I suppose it would be hoping too much to ask if there is any particular lady involved at the moment, sir?'

His chief moved his papers around.

'There is Lady Waterman, of course. She lives at the London address. I'll give it to you in a minute. There is also another woman. She and Sir Francis have been—um—associating for many years. Her name is Angela Dunning, and you'll certainly need to talk to her. There are probably others, there always have been. Mostly, they are brief interludes, and not the kind that would lead anyone to murder. But you will naturally have to explore the possibility.'

'How much time have I got, sir?'

'Three days' was the uncompromising rejoinder. 'That's the longest I can delay the inquest without provoking the Press. I realise it isn't long, but you'll have to do what you can.'

Three days. It was impossible, reflected Bradman sourly. They must have known that when they picked him.

'Where do I start, sir?'

'Start with this general practitioner, Mellows. Good chap, from what I'm told. He has first-hand knowledge of the scene of death, for one thing, and you needn't be too cagey with him, for another. In a way, you have him to thank for the assignment.'

Oh, have I? reflected Bradman. I must remember to thank him very much.

'Now, before you set off, we'll just go

through these notes together. Bring your chair up closer.'

Bradman pulled his chair up to the table, and they both bent their heads.

CHAPTER FOUR

Lawrence Mellows looked at his visitor with misgivings. He had expected someone more mature, someone of at least his own age. Perhaps these people weren't taking him very seriously. The Chief Constable himself had said he would have to pass the matter upwards. Mellows had no clear idea of what that meant, nor of what kind of man it could be expected to produce, but it certainly was not this smooth-faced young man who had introduced himself as Bradman.

Still, mustn't give offence.

'I suppose the rest of your team will be hard at it in other quarters, eh?'

Bradman smiled to himself. The doctor had not said 'including your boss', but that was what was implied. People always seemed to expect some grizzled, silver-haired savant at times like this.

'The team, Doctor,' he replied slowly, 'sits before you. The P.M. thought this was a job for one man only.'

He had no authority to quote the Prime Minister, and it was very much to be doubted whether the head of the state had ever heard of him, or ever would but that was something the doctor had no way of checking.

The effect was all he could have wished.

The casual reference to the Prime Minister hit Mellows like a douche of cold water. One could scarcely get more upwards than the Prime Minister. And, of course, there were some brilliant young people around these days. Brilliant. This chap Bradman, for instance. If they had given him a task of this importance, and left him single-handed, he was clearly a man to watch.

'Then you've a great deal to get through, Mr Bradman,' he said, in a more conciliatory tone. 'I'll try not to waste your time.'

'Cause of death, then,' queried Bradman. 'Has it been possible to identify the poison yet?'

That was a sore point with Mellows.

'You'd have to ask your own pathology people about that,' he huffed. 'They refuse to divulge anything to me at all. A bit cool, in my opinion, considering they were my samples.'

'Routine, Doctor,' he was assured smoothly. 'the blanket has been dropped over everyone and everything connected with Sir Francis' unfortunate death. I am sure no one appreciates this better than you, since it was your foresight and, may I say, extremely good judgement which made it possible for this affair to be kept away from the public. We are all indebted to you for that.'

Dr Mellows preened himself. Chap was quite right, of course, nothing else the authorities could do. This Bradman seemed to have a pretty fair grasp of things.

The questioning resumed.

'Leaving aside then the exact nature of the poison, is there any question in your mind as to how it was administered?'

What did he mean, 'how it was administered'?

'Don't quite follow you.'

'What I mean is, there are three main ways in which a person can be poisoned. The most normal method is via the mouth. But there is also injection, and even the inhalation of poison gas.'

'Ah, see what you mean. Mouth. No question of it.'

Bradman paused.

'You seem very positive.'

'That's because I am. Absolutely. Thought about the possibility of an injection, and examined the body with that particularly in mind. Not just for the usual arm pricks, you understand. I really examined him. Remembered a case once where the needle went in under a toe-nail, so I left nothing to chance. As for gas, no. There is no mistaking the signs when a person has inhaled noxious fumes.'

Good, thought Bradman. For the moment, at least, he could afford to discount injection and gas.

'So we are speaking of the most ordinary method. Tell me, for a person to be poisoned in that way, would it necessarily mean that the poison had been taken very recently?'

'Ah.'

Mellows sat back, and composed his hands. It was the pose he always assumed at question time with students, although he was unaware of it.

'To answer you in one word, no. However, I ought to elaborate on that.'

'If you would be good enough.'

Bradman had no objection to the lecturer technique. He was, after all, a student for all practical purposes.

'For our purposes,' commenced the doctor, 'we need only concern ourselves about the time-factor. There is no such thing as a delayed-action poison which can be taken orally. In other words, nothing which will take several days to do its work. What you can have is a build-up process. What I mean by that is, poison can be introduced into the system in small doses over a period. This accumulates to a point where the system can no longer tolerate the alien substance, and the result is death. A favourite method with poisoners over the years, but I think we can discount it.'

Oh, do you? reacted Bradman.

'Discount it, Doctor? Why do you say that?'

Mellows had been expecting the question, invited it almost. He'd had many hours to think about his distinguished corpse, and formed certain conclusions of his own.

'The build-up of a lethal dose requires a closed-in situation. The victim has to be a person of fixed routine, with normal daily comings and goings. The murderer has to be someone in close and regular contact with those events. In other words, they should ideally live in the same house, or at least be in attendance on the victim at pre-set intervals. The most obvious murderer would be the victim's spouse, but a domestic servant, such as a cook or a butler, could conceivably have the same opportunity.'

'Then Sir Francis was surely vulnerable?' queried Bradman. 'He had a wife, and grown children. He also had a housekeeper down here.'

'Mrs Cooper? Yes, that's all true. But the man's lifestyle is incompatible with the required technique. No one could be quite certain where he would be, from one day to the next. Quite often, he couldn't even control his activities himself. If some situation were to develop, he could quite easily find himself needed at the other end of the country at a few hours' notice. Or even overseas, that's been known. What Sir Francis would have considered his routine, had he been asked, would have seemed more like a nightmare to the average man. As for his eating habits, they would undoubtedly drive a dietitian to drink. A banquet in some northern city in the evening, a quick breakfast on a train back to

London. Probably a pub sandwich in the middle of the day. Something on a tray late at night when he got home. If he wasn't called off somewhere else, meantime. The man would be attended and served by a dozen different people every day. In the absence of some national conspiracy, I think you must reject the idea.'

Bradman was pleasantly surprised. This man Mellows had clearly given the matter a lot of consideration, and his conclusions had a sound ring to them. This could save him a lot of time.

'That's a very nice piece of deduction, if you don't mind my saying so, Doctor. And it sounds like sense to me. So, what are we left with? Just one dose of poison, and administered not too long before death?'

Lawrence Mellows' face was grave when he replied.

'One dose, I would say yes to that. As to how recently it entered the system, that I could not say without knowing the substance involved. Your path people—'

He waved a hand in resignation.

'Quite so, Doctor. I'll take up the point with them. Well, I'd better be getting out to the house. What sort of a lady is Mrs Cooper? Easy to talk to, would you say?'

Mellows frowned.

'Hard to say. Obviously the poor woman wasn't at her best when we met. Not to be expected, considering the circumstances. Still, even making allowances, I found her not very forthcoming. The local people seem to think she's rather a distant sort of person. Not actively unfriendly, but the type who keeps herself to herself.'

'M'm. Well, I'll soon know. Thanks for all the help, Doctor, and we'll certainly be meeting again.'

Mellows walked with him to the door.

'I think there's one point you ought to make clear to your forensic experts,' he said finally. 'I shall be called upon as the examining physician at the inquest. That means I shall be under oath, as you appreciate. Since it seems I am not to be trusted with the results of their findings, I shall require a report from them, stating that the tests were negative. It's the only way I can testify with a clear conscience.'

Dear me, the poor man really was upset by being excluded. The departing Bradman contrived not to grin at this little outburst.

'Quite understand, Doctor. I'll make the position clear to them.'

* * *

Ten minutes later, his car scrunched to a halt in the gravel driveway of Sir Francis Waterman's house. Considering the status of the occupant, it wasn't a very big establishment. Five bedrooms, probably, he estimated, and as many rooms again downstairs. Pretty though, with the ivy and honeysuckle climbing all over the outer walls.

A uniformed sergeant stood outside the front door, watching his approach. Sergeant Austin, Curly to his friends, was surprised to see that the important visitor was, if anything, younger than himself. Carried it well, though, bit of authority in his bearing, and so on. Even so, considering the emphasis placed on the need to give this Mr Bradman every possible co-operation, Curly Austin would have expected someone older, civil-servant type, more studious-looking.

Bradman liked the look of the waiting man. He had an open, cheery face below the fair hair, and a general overweightness which suggested he ought to spend more time in the police gymnasium.

'Mr Bradman?'

'Yes. How do you do, Sergeant. Let's have a walk around the garden.'

When they were away from the house, Bradman said, 'What do you think of Mrs Cooper?'

The policeman was unprepared for the question.

'How do you mean?'

'I mean, what sort of a lady is she? What's her attitude to you, for instance? Some people get a bit edgy when they have policemen under their feet all the time.'

'Ah.' Austin considered for a moment. Then, 'A bit stand-offish, I would say. She's civil enough, but she keeps her distance. None of this "I've just made a nice cup of tea" business, not with her. Seems to spend most of her time in her own room. That's understandable, of course. The lady's very upset, you can see that. Oh, and she doesn't like us being inside the house. So far as she's concerned, we are here to keep out visitors, and we can do that just as well outside. I wouldn't be looking for a warm welcome if I were you.'

'Thanks for the warning. What about the visitors, by the way? Have you had any trouble with them?'

The sergeant shook his head.

'Only with the Press, and I expected that. Haven't been any others much. Just the vicar, and a lady from the village who came to see if she could do any shopping for Mrs Cooper. The daughter's here, of course. Arrived about an hour ago.'

'Mrs Cooper's daughter?'

'No. Sir Francis' girl. Melanie. The one who got divorced from that gambler bloke last year. Big fuss about it at the time.'

Bradman seemed to recall something about it.

'Yes, I know the one. What is she doing here?'

Austin shrugged.

'I wouldn't know, Mr Bradman. Some member of the family has to take charge, I suppose. I believe his wife won't be coming, not until the funeral, that is.'

This new development was unexpected, and unwelcome. Bradman did not like the idea of anyone going through Waterman's effects, daughter or no.

'Well, I'd better get inside. Lord knows what she's up to in there.'

As they walked briskly back to the house, the police officer said, 'Hope I didn't do wrong, Mr Bradman, letting her in? Didn't think I had any authority to stop her.'

He was clearly concerned, and Bradman hastened to reassure him.

'Nothing you could have done, Sergeant. Daughter of the deceased, and all that. Still, there are papers in there which are none of her concern, so I must keep them away from her. Which room is the study?'

They were at the front door again, and Sergeant Austin pointed. 'Second door on the left, off the hall.'

'Thank you. See you later.'

Bradman walked quickly through the carpeted hallway and knocked on the study door, opening it at the same time. A young woman was bent over the desk, and she turned as he entered.

'Don't you usually wait to be asked?' she demanded. 'Who are you, anyway?'

She was tall, this one. Five nine or even ten. Shiny, straight black hair was pulled back behind small ears, setting off the high cheekbones and strong jawline. The nose was a little too large for perfection, but all in all, Melanie Waterman, or whatever her surname now was, came into the knock-out category. Or would, Bradman amended, without the hostile twist to the red lips and the unfriendliness flashing from hazel eyes.

'My name is Bradman, and I am from the Home Office,' he said smoothly. 'I have been sent here to take charge of Sir Francis' confidential papers. You're his daughter, aren't you? How do you do.'

This information did nothing to change her expression. 'Home Office,' she echoed. 'Take charge? You'll touch nothing here. This is a private house. You can't just come barging in to someone's home, giving orders. It's not a police state yet, you know.'

The reaction was no more than Bradman would have expected in the circumstances. But it was the tone of her voice that puzzled him. There was something else there, apart from outrage. Fear? Anxiety? He couldn't be certain.

'Believe me, I shall do everything in my power to avoid intruding, and please accept my condolences.'

The words were conciliatory, but his attitude remained uncompromising. The girl straightened up, measuring him with hostile eyes.

'You can take your condolences with you as you leave,' she advised him finally.

'Which will not be until I have completed my business here,' he replied firmly. 'I will disturb you as little as possible, Miss Waterman.'

'My name isn't Waterman,' she snapped, 'at least I'm rid of that handicap. I'm Mrs Nicos. What was your name, again?'

Nicos. Yes, that was it. A few more details about her divorce case filtered back into his recollection.

'Bradman, Mrs Nicos. I have my identification here, if you would care to—'

'You can shove that along with your condolences,' she told him rudely. 'You're too big for me to chuck out, but luckily there's a rather well-built policeman outside. We'll see what he can do.'

Crossing to the door, she stepped outside calling, 'Sergeant? Would you come here please?'

Sergeant Austin came quickly, noting the contrast between the set face of the girl and the imperturbable calm of the man.

'Yes, miss? Something I can do ?'

Melanie nodded emphatically.

'If you would be so kind,' she said with heavy sarcasm. 'This person is an intruder here. Would you kindly evict him from the premises, preferably using force.'

Austin lowered his gaze in case there should be an unwelcome twinkle in his eye.

'I'm afraid I have no authority to do that, madam. Mr Bradman is here in an official capacity.'

'Oh, can't you,' she replied furiously. 'Well then, I'd better get hold of someone who can. What's your inspector's name?'

The sergeant shook his head.

'The inspector won't be able to help you, madam. Nor will the superintendent. In fact, I doubt whether the Chief Constable himself could countermand Mr Bradman's authority.'

She stared at him in disbelief.

'The Chief Constable?' she repeated incredulously. 'Are you telling me that the Chief Constable of the county can't shift—this clerk?'

Austin coughed delicately.

'This gentleman is no clerk, madam, believe me.' Then he turned to the listening man. 'Is everything in order, Mr Bradman? Did you wish me to take—er—any other steps?'

What he was plainly asking was whether Melanie Nicos needed to be restrained. They'd known what they were about when they sent Sergeant Austin on this job, reflected Bradman.

'Thank you, Sergeant. I don't think we need detain you any longer. I'm sure Mrs Nicos now has a clearer picture of the situation.'

Melanie's head swung from one of the other as the reality of the position dawned on her.

'I was wrong, it seems. We do have a police state after all.'

'Please come and sit down for a moment, Mrs Nicos,' suggested Bradman. 'I am sure if we talk calmly we can soon clear the air.'

He nodded his thanks to Austin, who went away.

Melanie stood for a moment, undecided, then walked back inside, slammed the door, and flumped down in a chair.

'This had better be good,' she said ominously.

CHAPTER FIVE

The seated girl was watching with furious eyes as Bradman crossed the room and made himself comfortable. For all her display of outrage, Melanie Nicos was extremely apprehensive. She had had every right to complain about this man's intrusion, and her reaction had been no more than might reasonably have been expected in the circumstances. But it was more than her bereavement and grief that had been affronted. Self-interest had been her prime motive in trying to get rid of the newcomer. She needed more time alone in the house, and her reasons went far beyond those of the grieving daughter. When she realised she was not going to get any assistance from the police, her apprehension had deepened.

Bradman's youth did nothing to lessen the feeling.

Had he been older, she could more readily have accepted the deference shown to him by Sergeant Austin. It was normal to associate authority with grey hair. The fact that Bradman bore authority at his age only made him the more dangerous in her eyes. She had seen young men in high places before, in that other world of her ex-husband's, and knew the type well. Such men were extra clever, extra ambitious, and she recognised the signs in this—this what? Government investigator, or what was he?

Well, whatever he was, there was one thing certain. He was a ruthless bastard, or he wouldn't be where he was at his age. She would have to play the suffering relative bit for all it was worth.

Bradman was unhurried in his movements. The girl puzzled him. It was only natural that she should resent him, in the circumstances, but there was something else. Something besides the near-hysteria of a bereaved daughter. He couldn't put his finger on it, and was organising his mind so as to bring it to bear on this unknown quantity.

'Mrs Nicos,' he began, 'you could be of great assistance to me, and I would very much appreciate your co-operation.'

Melanie eyed him narrowly. Surely he wasn't going to try the helpless little boy approach? She'd seen more helpless Alsatian dogs.

'Doing what?' she queried flatly.

'Let me explain what I'm doing here,' he said smoothly. 'Your father was a prominent man, a man whose every move was a matter of great interest to everyone. He was active in a dozen different areas, always at a high level, and his passing is going to be a very real loss.'

She inclined her head, wondering where all this was leading. He was talking like an editorial in a newspaper, so far.

'Sir Francis was naturally in touch with important people, in many spheres of life. He was privy to all kinds of restricted material, knew which way thinking was being shaped in many quarters, and was indeed playing his own part, making his own important contributions on a wide variety of subjects.'

Restricted material? Was that what this was all about? Was this Bradman some kind of security man?

'From the way you're talking,' she observed carefully, 'you sound like some kind of spy, come to recover the plans or something. Is that what you're doing here?'

Bradman permitted himself a small smile of denial.

'Please hear me out,' he insisted. 'You can't fail to know what happens these days, when someone as well known as your father dies. He leaves behind enemies. People who would like to see him discredited. Some of these people are merely being spiteful, seeking revenge for some personal slight in the past. Others have motives which are far more important. They want to have doubt cast on the man's work, on his integrity. It is not a personal matter at all, in fact they could easily be people who liked him as a man.'

'Then what—'

'Please. As I say, such people are not especially interested in the man. But their interests were being affected by the work he was doing, the committees he sat on, the enquiries he conducted, things of that nature. If they can somehow blacken the character of the man, it is a comparatively simple matter to transfer some of that distrust to what he was doing. To undermine the value of his work. Am I making myself clear?'

Despite herself, Melanie was interested in what he was saying.

'I think so,' she replied. For one thing, my father is on this Public Spending thing at the moment. Or was, I should say. That committee has already upset a lot of people with its findings, and there is a lot more to come, so we're told. What you're suggesting is, if someone could produce something nasty about Father, it could be used to show the kind of people who sat on the committee, to make the public think their findings weren't worth listening to.' She leaned forward, tapping at the inside of her palm. 'I can see that. If Father had been messing about with small boys in public lavatories, people would react against anything associated with him. That's what you're saying, isn't it?'

Bradman tried not to show any surprise at the nature of the example she had chosen.

'Yes,' he agreed. 'You are being a little extreme, perhaps, but yes, that is the kind of thing I mean.'

The girl half-smiled.

'Oh, don't worry, my dear father was not interested in the choirboys. It was their mothers who had to watch out. You know about the whore, of course?'

A man either had to resign himself to her direct way of speaking, or waste a lot of time looking confused.

'What whore?'

'Dear Angela. Everybody knows about Angela. Angela Dunning?'

She put the name to him as a question. He kept his face composed as he parried.

'I don't think I know of the lady. You'd better tell me, now that you've started.'

'There are some cigarettes in my bag. It's on the desk behind you. Would you mind tossing them over?'

After a moment's hesitation, he turned round and located the bag, an expensive grey crocodile affair, and opened it. There was a packet of cigarettes near the top of the assorted female bric-à-brac. As he lifted them clear he saw something else. Half-hidden by a scrap of linen, which was presumably supposed to be a handkerchief, lay a miniature pearl-handled revolver. He decided not to mention it at the moment, and passed over the cigarettes.

'Thanks,' said Melanie carelessly. 'Want one?'

He took one of the extra-long filter-tips and produced his lighter. He ought to have looked more closely at the packet, he realised. They were menthol-flavoured. Horrible.

'Now then, Mrs Nicos—'

'I'm not too fond of that name,' she snapped. 'Why don't you call me Melanie? It's pretty ridiculous, if we're going to be dissecting the old man's private life, for us to try being formal with each other. What am I going to call you? Don, I suppose.'

Strange girl, this. All bristly, to start with. Then, as if she had come to some kind of decision, suddenly handing out cigarettes, and exchanging first names.

'It isn't my name,' he demurred, 'but people do tend to call me that.'

She grinned, obviously interested.

'And are you any good at it? Cricket, that is?'

'No,' he confessed. 'I'm no great credit to the name in that direction.'

'Good,' she decided. 'It's a boring game anyway.'

He wondered whether her normal conversational style took this erratic form, or whether she simply wanted to change the subject.

'You were going to tell me about Angela Dunning,' he reminded her.

'So I was. No great secret, really. She and my father have had this long-standing affair. Must be about fifteen years now. That's why Mother won't live with him. She turns out, of course, if he needs formal support at some public function, but that's as far as it goes.'

'I see. An odd set-up, if you don't mind my saying so. Is there any particular reason why there should not have been a divorce? I mean, fifteen years is hardly a spur-of-the-moment kind of relationship.'

Melanie nodded, looking around for an ash-tray.

'You'd have to know my ma to understand that. She comes from the same background as the old man. Grinding poverty, and all that. She had helped him during twenty years of their marriage, before Angela cropped up. She had worked just as hard as he had, was at least half-responsible for his position in the world. As far as she was concerned, she wasn't going to be chucked on one side, just because he'd used her up. If he wanted a divorce, there wouldn't be any quiet covering-up. There would be hell to pay, and Francis Waterman M.P. could kiss his career goodbye. Well, she knew him all right. He couldn't risk that, Angela or no. So, it's just sort of carried on like that, all these years.'

Bradman was beginning to think he did not especially like Sir Francis Waterman.

'So Miss Dunning has lived, what's the expression, in the shadows, for fifteen years.'

'Yes,' agreed Melanie. 'Matter of fact, you can't help feeling a bit sorry for the poor bitch, in some ways. She's quite a nice woman really, and the old man's given her a lousy time of it. Just like my mother all over again, really.'

'In what way?'

Melanie curled her lip.

'In the same way. Perfect bastard where the women are concerned, my dear pater. Couldn't keep his hands off them. Office girls, waitresses, other people's wives, they were all open season to the old man. Oh, I expect Angela has suffered just as much as my mother, only she hasn't got the proud distinction of being married to him.'

Bradman put on a look of polite enquiry.

'I don't suppose you could help with Miss Dunning's address?'

'Somewhere in Kensington,' replied the girl. 'Should find it here I would imagine. On his desk, probably.'

The investigator nodded. This was a good opening.

'I expect you're right. The more personal stuff will be close to hand. What was it you were looking for, Mrs—er—Melanie?'

She looked startled.

'Why, I—looking for? How do you mean, looking for?'

'You were searching for something when I came in. Something quite specific, I would say.'

Her mouth set in a grim line.

'You can imagine what you please,' she said tightly. 'I was simply going through his things.

Mother asked me to. You can check with her if you want to.'

No, he reflected, there would be little point in doing that. Mother would support daughter, and, in any case, it could be true. There might be something there they both wanted. It was time for the friendly policeman act.

'Look, Melanie, let me explain the position to you,' he suggested. 'As of this moment, everything in which Sir Francis was involved is frozen. No papers, however personal, will be overlooked, and nothing released, until it has been cleared. That includes family matters, I'm afraid.'

'And they call this a free country,' she scoffed. 'Anybody would think Hitler was back.'

'However,' he pursued, 'the initial responsibility rests with me. It is for me to judge what needs further attention. Why don't you try trusting me? Tell me what you want. Remember I'm going to find it anyway. If I know it's of special interest to you, and at the same time is not relevant to what I'm doing here, it's just conceivable I could let you have it.'

Melanie was thinking rapidly. She didn't go for all that jazz about trusting this man. She knew a tough egg when she saw one. All the same, what he said did make sense. He was going to find it anyway, and if he did the wrong thing, the balloon really could go up.

‘How do I know I can trust you?’ she demanded.

‘You don’t,’ he returned, ‘but what have you got to lose? To me, as things stand, it will be just another piece of paper, or document, or whatever. I might make the wrong decision, so far as you are concerned. At least, if I know of your interest, I shall make a conscious decision. It may still go against you, but you will have tried. Now then, what do you say?’

What I am tempted to say, my boy, is that you are a smooth-talking bastard, but that might not be very politic in the circumstances. No. This is more a situation for the trusting little woman bit.

She said half-sadly, ‘Devil and the deep, really, isn’t it? I mean, I don’t seem to have a lot of choice.’

Bradman made no reply, contenting himself with waiting, while she composed herself. Then she spoke again.

‘Very well. It’s about my dear ex-husband, Alex Nicos.’

‘Ah. What about him?’

‘You know who he is?’ she countered.

The man opposite scoured his mind for information. Nicos was a well-known London figure, a gambler on a huge scale, and also a man with various business interests of a fringe nature. There’d been a lot of rumbling in the Press at the time of his divorce from this attractive, headstrong woman. All the sympathy had been for the daughter of the well-loved Sir Francis Waterman.

'I only know what I have read in the newspapers,' he admitted. 'Mr Nicos seems to be a man of considerable wealth, a variety of interests, and frequently features in the society pages.'

Melanie's expression was sour.

'He is also a considerable shit,' she added venomously. 'You left that out.'

'I never met the gentleman,' contributed Bradman calmly.

'Lucky you.' She ground out her cigarette angrily. 'We weren't married very long, you know. Just long enough for me to find out how the women must expect to be treated if they marry primitives. I wanted rid of him and his charming little habits as fast as ever possible, and I got out. Unfortunately, Alex turned nasty. Believe me, with a man like that, nasty takes on new depths. He let me understand that while he may not be able to prevent me legally, I would always be his property so far as he was concerned. He would also see to it that no other man would ever be attracted to me.'

'Oh?' Bradman was surprised. 'And what on earth gave him a stupid idea like that?'

'He intended to disfigure me,' she said, very slowly. 'Oh, not personally. He's too clever to be caught for anything like that. He has—people. People who do little errands for him. Believe me, you don't know Mr Nicos when things don't go his way.'

Bradman was trying to evaluate the truth of what she was saying. She certainly seemed to believe it.

'But that was a year ago, if I remember,' he pointed out. 'He doesn't seem to have made much progress with your disfigurement.'

'That's because of my father. I went to him, to see if there was anything he could do. Say what you like about the old man, he was up to all the tricks. Well, he wasn't going to take a thing like that lying down. He put out some feelers, and he really hit the jackpot. Dear Alex was already married to some unfortunate creature in Greece. There had never been a divorce, and so our marriage was a non-starter from the beginning. But that wasn't all. His name isn't Nicos at all, it's something quite different. That means that every deal he's mixed up in, every document he's signed as Nicos, is worthless. So there you have it, Don. That's what I was looking for. I want those papers in my own hands so that Alex doesn't get the idea that my father's death changes anything.'

It was quite a story. Bradman sat, musing over the implications of what he had just been told.

'I'm not doubting the truth of what you say,' he began carefully, 'but why didn't your father act as soon as he had this evidence? It would have been a simple enough matter.'

She wasn't offended, he noted with relief.

'That's true, it would, if he were only after Alex. That wasn't his basic purpose. What he wanted was to ensure my safety. Once he blew the whistle, Alex would be out of control. Nothing has changed in that direction. I only want those papers for my own safety, and not to expose Mr Bloody Nicos. So-called.'

What Melanie had no way of knowing was that she had just provided her listener with a first-class motive for someone wanting her father out of the way, together with a prime suspect for the rôle of murderer. He also did not see how he could release such important documents to the girl. One thing he could do, was to set her mind at rest.

'Melanie, I appreciate your trust in telling me all this. In return, I can make you a certain promise. But I'm taking an awful chance in doing it. In fact, I'm trusting you.'

This was a new departure, and she was intrigued to know what was coming next.

'Trusting me to do what?'

He looked into her eyes, and his tone was grave.

'I am trusting you not to repeat one word of what we have said here this morning. It would be denied, even if you did, but it would be a great embarrassment to me. It would make me very unpopular in certain quarters.'

'But you haven't said anything yet,' she pointed out.

Bradman took a deep breath.

'True. Then I shall, now. Within the next few hours Mr Nicos will be receiving some visitors. They will explain to him that if anything untoward should happen to you then he should be aware that the same thing will happen to him. Only worse, much worse.'

Melanie's eyes were wide with surprise.

'You're serious, aren't you?'

'Very.'

'And you can really arrange such a thing? I mean, it's not exactly the game your namesake played, is it?'

'Neither is violence against women,' he said abruptly. 'Some of us don't much care for that sort of thing.'

'My God.'

She slumped back in the chair, at a loss for words. Then, 'I think I'm going to cry.'

I do hope not, thought Bradman desperately.

CHAPTER SIX

Lunch consisted of one roast beef sandwich and a half-pint of bitter. As he spread mustard on the second half of the round, Bradman was thinking over the events of the morning. So far, he'd been able to contact three of the people on the list supplied by Sir Edward. Dr Mellows, Melanie Nicos, and the housekeeper, Mrs Cooper.

Mrs Cooper had been as forthcoming as one could expect from a village woman. True enough, she had answered his questions, but she hadn't actually volunteered very much. He had found himself having to dig out every scrap of information, and not because she was unwilling to co-operate. He hadn't felt that. It was simply not in her nature to gossip, and this applied particularly to her late employer.

She had not been with him very long. Bradman's hopes of a faithful old retainer and friend had quickly been dashed. Sir Francis had only bought the place a few months previously, with an eye to his ultimate retirement. He did not spend a great deal of time at the house, often arriving unannounced. Sometimes he would stay for the night, and on other occasions he might remain for three or four days. His movements were unpredictable, and governed, according to Mrs Cooper, by some dark forces referred to throughout the discussion as 'them'. Sir Francis, poor man, couldn't call his soul his own, it would seem. He never knew what 'they' might want of him next. It wasn't right, it wasn't, that such a lovely man should be at their beck and call day and night. Weekends included. A man of his age ought to be entitled to a bit of peace now and then, not being made to go gallivanting all over the place at a moment's notice. Well, she hoped they were satisfied now. She'd always maintained they would kill him in the end, and now it was done. Somebody was going to have to answer for that, and it was no more than they deserved.

Bradman had almost lost his calm detachment when the lady made this observation. Then it dawned on him that she was not referring to the apprehension of his poisoner. Mrs Cooper was hinting darkly at the Final Accounting, when Sir Francis' unknown persecutors would be called upon to explain their actions.

By careful questioning, which entailed the avoidance of anything like the approach of an interrogator, Bradman had contrived to piece together the events of the final evening.

Sir Francis had arrived at about three-thirty in the afternoon, announcing an overnight stay, and saying that he had to work on some papers for the following day. Bradman had already found these papers, and knew they related to a trade union meeting. His next call, in fact, was to be at the union headquarters, to see the General Secretary, Len Bowman.

The great man had a cup of tea in his study, after changing his clothes, and remained there until dinner was ready. Bradman was keenly interested in what he had to eat, and luckily that was one subject where Mrs Cooper was prepared to expand. She had been concerned, lest anyone might think her cooking had in any way contributed to the heart attack. It appeared that she had a down on animal fats, as being unhealthy, and no one could accuse her of presenting fried food to her employer. On that evening she had prepared one of his favourite dishes, a strong curry. No, she did not share the meal. Couldn't stand the stuff, as was well known locally. There had been some chaff in the village shop when she first purchased the raw materials for her new employer, it being a by-word in the village that Mrs Cooper would have no truck with any of that foreign muck. They were accustomed now to her regular order, which was a labour of love, so far as she was concerned. She opened every available window on curry nights, to get the smell out of the house.

She had prepared the meal herself, and there was no one else in the house but Sir Francis. No, he hadn't had any visitors that afternoon or evening, and it was not possible for anyone to have come to the house without her knowledge. The kitchen faced down the driveway, and she could not be mistaken.

It had to be the curry of course, decided Bradman. Whatever killed Sir Francis Waterman had been taken into his system through the mouth. He had had tea in the afternoon, which Mrs Cooper shared. Apart from his dinner, he could have drunk from the whisky bottle in his study, the contents of which were under analysis. But the curry was the obvious source. It would be the ideal covering taste for the addition of some extra ingredient. The problem was to see how it had been administered. Mrs Cooper was adamant that no one else could have had access to the food, or even to the house itself. That meant only two people could be responsible. The dead man was one, and Mrs Cooper was the other. Yet Bradman couldn't bring himself to accept her as a candidate. She hardly knew the man, for a start. For another thing, the lady was not the type to have caused Sir Francis to make any of his famous sexual overtures, being little short of repellent in her physical make-up. Apart from those factors, she had behaved in an extraordinary way for anyone under suspicion, going to great lengths to prove that no one else could possibly have had an opportunity to kill the man. Scarcely the attitude of a person with something to hide.

Bradman was too experienced, despite his age, to dismiss Mrs Cooper entirely from his mind, but he was prepared to discount her for the immediate present. What he wanted was a motive, and that she seemed clearly to lack. He drove slowly through the village on his way back to London. All this was going through his mind, yet at the same time he couldn't erase the image of Melanie Nicos from it. Those lovely, haunted eyes had really reached out to him, and if he weren't so heavily involved with Veronica Broadhurst, he would have had to do something about them. He had had a feeling that he wouldn't be too quickly rebuffed in that direction. Ah well, no time to think about that now.

It was five to two, and Len Bowman had said he would see him at two o'clock. Leaving the pub, he walked briskly round the corner, and presented himself at the union offices. There had been a great outcry, years before, when the union had decided to spend half a million pounds on new premises. Public meetings, vitriolic editorials, and special reports on the television news. Now, the decision seemed to have been justified. The half-million investment had grown into a ten million pound asset, and there were few dissenters any longer.

Bowman received him at once, rising from the chair behind his plain wooden desk to shake hands.

'Bit young, aren't you?' he greeted. 'Charlie Bolt said this was important. It better be. I've got a rough meeting coming up at half-past two.'

Directness had always been a hallmark of the celebrated Len Bowman, the visitor reminded himself.

'I'll be as quick as I can, Mr Bowman—'

'Call me Len,' was the curt interruption. '"Mr" is for managers. I'm not one of them.'

Bradman did not choose to argue the point. It flashed through his mind that a man with the responsibility for two million members, and capital assets running into many millions of pounds, was a manager on a grand scale. But this was not the time for a discussion of that kind.

'Len, then,' he amended. 'I'm Don, by the way. I'm here about Sir Francis Waterman's death.'

'Are you now?' Bowman squinted at him. 'What about it?'

The pale blue eyes seemed to bore into Bradman's head, and he was thankful he had rehearsed his story thoroughly.

'What I'm going to tell you has to remain between us,' he said seriously. 'You will appreciate the need, the national need, when I explain.'

'National need?' repeated his listener. 'Well, I don't know so much about that. Different people have different ideas about what that might mean.'

'Yes, they do,' acknowledged Bradman. 'But

in this instance, Charlie Bolt himself has given his agreement. His unqualified agreement. Please telephone him for confirmation, if you wish.'

'No need for that. We've talked once. That's enough.'

Len Bowman had an inborn suspicion of all officials, even including those appointed from his own ranks. They got involved in systems and procedures, lost sight of main issues, in a welter of paper work and regulations. This young chap was an official of some kind, that much was plain. Unusual type, though, you had to admit that. Couldn't see this fellow carrying an umbrella, or catching the eight-sixteen every morning. The rummest thing about this visitor was his age. The way Charlie Bolt had built him up, you'd have expected somebody who was at least pushing sixty. This fellow wasn't even thirty. Yet, he must have the credentials, or Charlie wouldn't have spoken so plain. Give him whatever he wants, that's what Charlie had said, and Charlie Bolt was the last man in the world to knuckle under to any of these Whitehall poofters.

'The fact is,' began the subject of all this scrutiny, 'that a certain brief-case is missing. Sir Francis had it with him at lunch-time yesterday. Some time between then and the time of his death, the brief-case became—mislaid.'

'Pinched, you mean? What was in it?'

Bradman wished people would not interrupt, so that he could develop a story along logical lines.

'You raise two points there, Len. It is not to be ruled out that the case was stolen, but it could just as easily have been left somewhere. The point is, we don't know, and that's a matter for grave concern. So far as your second question goes, we also don't know what it contained. I see by your face that I need not stress the seriousness of the situation.'

'You need not, son. By God you needn't.'

Bowman was all attention now, and the investigator pressed home his advantage.

'Now then, the purpose of my coming here. It's twofold. First of all, I am to warn you of the possibility that confidential documents are missing, so that you may take whatever steps you think appropriate to defend your position, if that should be necessary. Secondly, I am going to ask you to guess what those documents might be.'

'Hm.'

That was all right, the first part. There could well have been papers relevant to today's meeting, for one thing. That was the hottest item on the immediate horizon, so far as the union was concerned. What Len Bowman didn't care for was the idea of telling this outsider what it was all about. He only hoped Charlie Bolt knew what he was doing.

'What will you do with this information?' he

queried.

'Probably nothing. I shan't even pass it on, in all probability,' was the calm rejoinder. 'Whatever you tell me, I am to assess. If I think the information, in the wrong hands, can be used to discredit the country, the government or the trade union movement, then I will report upwards. If not, as I said just now, the matter is at an end.'

Bowman listened to this with a keen ear, reminding himself continually of what Charlie Bolt had said. This chap Bradman couldn't have left the university more than five years, and yet here he was, with an obviously high authority clearance. He was only confirmed in his earlier assessment that this was no ordinary official.

'Strictly confidential?'

'Absolutely.'

Bowman took a deep breath, and plunged in.

'All right then. Frank had a draft plan for the reorganisation of this union. New form of representation, everything. He and I were the only two with all the details. It's on the agenda for this afternoon. It might not sound a lot to an outsider, but believe me, there'll be bloody uproar once it's made public.'

The visitor considered for a moment, then said, 'Uproar within your own ranks, primarily?'

'Yes. There'll be side-effects elsewhere, you

can bet, but as you say, primarily it's a family matter.'

Bradman closed his eyes, thinking.

'Then, if it's on the agenda for today, there's not much use anyone could make of the papers. It's all about to come out, anyway. Presumably there'll be opposition?'

The man behind the desk laughed mirthlessly.

'Opposition? Nice way of putting it. There'll be bleeding hell to pay, that's what there'll be. But they'll know soon enough. I don't see what good that draft would be to anybody else. From your point of view, I'd say there's nothing to worry about.'

Phrasing the next question carefully, in order not to raise the suspicions of the agile-minded man opposite, Bradman asked, 'As a matter of interest, could Sir Francis' absence cause the plan to be defeated? I mean, if there is opposition, and it comes to a vote, could his absence cause a rejection, or a stalemate even?'

Anxious to leave no avenue unexplored, Bradman was probing to find out whether someone opposed to the scheme might have been driven to the extent of murder, in order to defeat it. Feelings in such matters could run very high, in his experience. It was a relief to see Len Bowman shaking his head.

'No chance of that,' he refuted. 'Just to be on the safe side, I've got Georgie Wading here to balance things up. No. We'll get it through. It'll be a rough do, especially without Frank, but we shall win. Er—it's almost twenty past.'

'Yes, I think I've got all I need. Thank you for your time, Len. I think you described it very accurately. This is a family matter. I don't see any need for me to bother you any further.'

Len Bowman stood up, to walk him to the door. On the point of leaving, the younger man turned.

'Oh, and one other little thing. Very personal, really. My masters don't want a lot of muck-raking in the Press. I know about Sir Francis' little weakness, where the ladies are concerned. Is there any particular lady here, that you know of, who might be in a position to cause any difficulties?'

Cunning sod, thought Bowman. Keeping that till right at the last. Well, he had an answer for him.

'I know what you mean, Don, and I'd be lying if I said otherwise. There was trouble of that sort a few years ago. One of our telephone girls, nice little thing. We had to jump on that one, telephone girl of all people. I mean, just imagine the sort of stuff that goes through our switchboard. We had to get rid of her, of course. And we told Frank straight. Any more of it and we'd let the newspapers have everything we knew against him. If he wanted his bits of spare he could look elsewhere. Never been any trouble from him since.'

Bradman nodded knowingly.

'Yes, I think I heard something about that young woman. A Miss Earnshaw, wasn't it?'

The general secretary shook his head, grinning.

'Wrong girl. That must have been some other cupboard you opened. Earnshaw, you say? Not one of ours, no. This one's name was Ryan. Maudie Ryan.'

'Oh, my mistake. Well, thanks again, Len. And good luck with your—um—' the door was standing open—'with your plans for this afternoon.'

He walked out of the building, passing a perspiring man whom he recognised as George Wading. If he was hot already, he'd be in a perfect lather by the end of the day, he reflected.

Outside, he walked to the nearest public telephone box, feeling in his pocket for coins. Tapping out a number, he made quick contact, and spoke urgently to the man at the other end.

Finally he said, 'Just checking the name once more. Ryan. Maude Ryan.'

CHAPTER SEVEN

Despite the fine afternoon the windows of the neat semi-detached house were firmly shut, and the curtains drawn. The man in the dark blue suit closed the gate carefully behind him and walked up the short pathway to the door. Pressing at a bell-push, he heard the first few notes of Good King Wenceslas echo somewhere inside, and waited.

After a while the door opened a mere crack, and a tall youth stood peering out at him.

'Yes?'

'Is Mrs Ludlow at home, please?'

'She's resting,' was the uncompromising reply.

'Ah. Well, I'm sorry to disturb her, but this is rather important.'

The youth bit his lip.

'You from the papers?'

'No, I have nothing to do with the Press, or any news service.'

'Well, who are you then?'

Bradman hesitated. It would be a simple matter for this boy to close the door on him, and he didn't want that.

'It's a personal matter,' he explained. 'Would you please tell her that I would like to see her. It concerns the death of Sir Francis Waterman.'

The young man's face indicated that he didn't know quite how to handle the situation. A voice called out, somewhere behind him, and he turned to listen.

'Just a minute,' he said, and closed the door.

A curtain twitched, and Bradman felt that he was being observed from inside. A further pause, and the door opened, wider this time.

'You can come in,' said the youth, awkwardly.

'Thank you.'

The narrow hallway was painted in bright colours, with a flowered carpet that shrieked beneath the feet. A large mirror also provided a shadowy picture of a Victorian music-hall scene, and a gaily coloured sombrero hung on a wall, with a pair of castanets placed exactly on either side. A pink lampshade dominated the ceiling, with gold tassels all around the fringe.

'In here.'

The youth pointed to a half-open door, and Bradman stepped in, tapping gently as he did so. A woman sat, watching his entrance. She was about fifty, with a pleasant face, marred at that moment by obvious grief.

'Mrs Ludlow?'

'Yes. Who are you, please?'

Her voice was controlled, as though she might be about to burst into further tears at any moment.

'My name is Bradman,' he announced

gently. 'I'm sorry to have to disturb you at a time like this, but there are one or two matters I think you can help with.'

'My son said it's about Frank. Sir Francis Waterman, that is. He was my cousin, you know. What was it you wanted?'

The visitor took a further step inside, conscious that the youth was standing behind him.

'I wonder if we might be alone, Mrs Ludlow,' he suggested. 'There are one or two points, rather confidential really.'

Grace Ludlow hesitated. Roy was all she had now, and she didn't want them to be divided. But there was something about this man, this Bradman, that told her she had better do as he asked.

'Roy, love, would you like to make us all a nice cup of tea? I expect Mr Bradman would like one.'

'That's very kind of you,' acknowledged the standing man.

Roy was uncertain.

'Will you be all right?'

'Course I will, love. Use the good cups, now.'

Roy went away, leaving the door ajar. Bradman closed it.

'May I sit down, Mrs Ludlow?'

'Oh dear, where are my manners. Yes, do. Please do. Will this take very long, Mr Bradman? I don't feel up to very much.'

There was another quality to her voice, besides grief. It could be anxiety, he thought.

'There are certain papers, rather important papers, which are missing from Sir Francis Waterman's office, Mrs Ludlow. It is imperative that they should be found, and we are exploring every possible avenue.'

She listened, nodding.

'You from his office, then?'

'No. I am from the Home Office,' he lied smoothly. 'At times like this it is part of our normal procedure to ensure that business continues.'

'But he wasn't in the government,' she objected. 'Not any more.'

Bradman had hoped that in such surroundings the mention of the Home Office would be sufficient. This woman was obviously not to be impressed too readily.

'Quite so,' he agreed, 'but you know how these things are, I'm sure. A prominent man like Sir Francis Waterman, whether he happens to be in or out of office at any particular time, is always active on matters of national importance. Almost, you might say, part of the establishment.'

He hoped he was striking the right note, and was relieved to see her head nodding.

'That's true enough. He always says—said, rather—that he didn't know when he had most to do. He was up to his ears just the same, whether he was government or opposition.

Always said that, Frank did.'

'You were very close, I believe?'

She smiled, and there was warmth in it.

'He was good to me, Frank was. And to the boy. Thinks the world of Frank, Roy does.'

'He seems like a fine young man,' rejoined Bradman. 'Sir Francis was a regular visitor, then?'

Mrs Ludlow pursed her lips.

'Well, not to say regular,' she demurred. 'I mean, you couldn't say he was here every Friday, on the dot of six, if that's what you mean. He was always popping in, though. Used to stay, sometimes. There's a spare room upstairs.

Bradman felt uncomfortable. He didn't very much relish his rôle of deceiving this pleasant, motherly woman.

'Did he not leave any papers here?'

She shook her head.

'Always very particular about that, Frank was. Do you know, he wouldn't even put his scrap paper in the dustbin? You never know, he used to say. Used to go down the garden and burn anything he didn't want. If it was raining, I've known him take his rubbish with him, sooner than trust the dustbin. Still, he knew best, I suppose.'

Bradman smiled inwardly. Evidently Mrs Ludlow had little idea of the importance of the 'scrap' paper, at the level of a man like Waterman.

'How long ago was his last visit?' he enquired casually.

'Oh, let me see, about a week. Yes. A week ago Monday it was. He's not been so much since he got this house in the country. Got to get it fixed up, you see.'

'Of course. And do you like the house?'

She looked surprised.

'Me? I've never been there. Don't expect to. Tell you the truth, I'm not even sure where it is, exactly. He did tell me, but it was some place I'd never heard of. Not far from Guildford, I do know that. Have you been there?'

'Yes, I have. It's a very pleasant spot.'

Roy came back into the room then, carrying a tray.

'Tea up,' he announced.

'Thank you, dear. Just just put it down there, will you? Mr Bradman and I won't be very long now.'

The youth set the tray down on the table, mildly surprised at the dismissal.

'Oh. Right then,' he said.

Bending over, he removed one of the brightly coloured cups and took it away with him.

'Don't mind Roy,' said his mother fondly. 'He's only making sure I'm all right.'

'He seems to look after you very well,' agreed Bradman. 'How old is he? Eighteen?'

'Seventeen,' she corrected. 'Doing his A

levels this year. Hope this doesn't upset his studies too much. They're very important, you know, A levels. Frank's always on at him. I mean, he always was—I mean—'

She caught her breath, and tears loomed in her eyes. Bradman stared into his cup.

'Young people are very resilient,' he offered kindly. 'I'm sure he'll do very well. Particularly since he knows it's important to you. Have you heard from Lady Waterman, Mrs Ludlow? No one seems to be quite certain where she is.'

At the mention of Waterman's widow, the face opposite changed. A look of reserve masked it.

'No,' was the short reply. 'We don't have anything to do with each other. We—er—we don't get on, you see.'

'Ah,' Bradman nodded understandingly. 'I see. But you'll meet at the funeral, of course.'

The headshake was quite firm.

'Shan't be going. Not Roy and me. It wouldn't be—we don't go where we're not wanted.'

Bradman set down his empty cup. There was only one thing left to be cleared up.

'Forgive my asking, Mrs Ludlow, but one of my duties is to ensure that there is no financial hardship in these cases. Even the most eminent men can be quite careless about their personal affairs. I believe Sir Francis was of some financial help to you. Are you going to be able to manage?'

She seemed surprised at first, then shrugged.

'Oh, you know about that, do you?' She looked at him with troubled eyes. 'I expect there's quite a lot you know, really, isn't there?'

Her hands were pulling nervously at the hem of her heavy dress as she spoke. When he replied, Bradman tried to make his tone soft and convincing.

'Please believe me, Mrs Ludlow, the last thing I want is to make you feel uncomfortable. You have nothing to fear, either now or in the future, from me. What I may or may not know, remains with me. I want you to believe that.'

She nodded tremulously, wanting it to be true.

'Thank you,' she said simply.

'Now then, what about your financial arrangements? There's this house to keep up, your son to maintain.'

'It'll be all right, I'm sure. He always said we'd be all right, if anything happened to him. There'll be insurance, or something. I expect the lawyers will be on to me.

'But there's no insurance policy here? He didn't leave it with you?'

She half-smiled.

'Lord, no. He wouldn't trust me with anything like that. I'm not very good with papers, you see. I'd probably use it for a shopping list, or something. No, that'll be somewhere safe, you can rely on that.'

He rose to go. Crossing over, he took her hands in his own.

'You're a very brave woman, Mrs Ludlow. You'll be all right, I'm certain. And as far as this visit goes, you need never give it another thought. Please don't bother to get up. I'll see myself out.'

Roy was lurking in the hallway. He straightened up when he saw that the visitor was about to leave.

'Everything all right?' he asked.

Bradman looked at him properly for the first time. Roy was tall, with fair tousled hair above an intelligent face. Nice-looking boy, he decided.

'Everything is all right,' he confirmed. 'Your mother is going to need all your support for a while.'

'Yes, I know,' was the rejoinder. 'I'll look after her.'

'I'm sure you will. Good luck, Roy.'

He went back outside then, with relief. Climbing into the car, he drove until he came to a park where children were playing a variety of ball-games. Pulling in, he sat and considered his recent visit.

Grace Ludlow had not seriously been in his mind as a possible murderess, but he had to see for himself. Now that he had made the trip, he was glad to have been able to confirm his original thoughts.

Despite his training, which insisted on total personal detachment, he found himself disliking Waterman more and more as his enquiries progressed. That unfortunate woman he'd just left had done nothing to improve his opinion.

It was only to be hoped that there really was an insurance policy, or some other financial arrangement, or that little world would collapse. Still. He brought himself back resolutely to the present. There was still much to be done, and little time to do it in.

CHAPTER EIGHT

When the doorbell rang, Detective Chief Superintendent Wilfred Hampton looked at his watch. This chap was punctual, a good start. On opening the door he was somewhat surprised at the visitor's youthful appearance. He'd known the man was young, but was not altogether prepared for the reality.

'I'm David Bradman,' announced the newcomer. 'Good of you to see me, Mr Hampton.'

'How do. Come on in. David, you say?'

Better strike the right note, he decided. Treat this chap as he would a new arrival from the police college.

'It is David, yes,' was the reply. 'But everyone calls me Don.'

'Don?'

Ah yes. Sir Donald, the great cricketer. Many was the time Hampton had sat enthralled, as he watched the Australian wizard perform. That was in Hampton's own youth, and the original Bradman was then at the end of his career, but still performing wonders.

As they went inside the house, Bradman was busy deciding on his approach. He'd sensed the rôle the senior policeman had elected for himself. The Chief Superintendent was taking up the stance of the eminence grise, the aged savant of the mountain-top, preparing to dole out wisdom to the young traveller. It was fair enough, he accepted, when one took into account the thirty years plus difference in their ages. In the past, he had found profit in adapting himself to the supplicant's rôle. And, he reminded himself, it was not entirely inappropriate to his visit.

'Would you like a drink? There's some Scotch.'

'No, thank you. This is one of those no-sleep assignments. I find I can keep going longer if I stick to coffee or tea. When the job is done, then I'll have several large drinks.'

He'd made the point in order to put his host's mind at rest. There were still a lot of people who mistrusted a man who didn't drink at all.

'Coffee, then,' decided Hampton. 'I keep the percolator permanently on the go in here. One advantage of living alone. You haven't got someone continually emptying the thing.'

He switched on the gleaming percolator, waving Bradman to a chair. Then he picked up his still-warm pipe and drew it back to life.

'I was a bit surprised to get your call, Don,' he announced. 'Rather thought I wouldn't hear any more about this business. Until I read something in the papers. What can I do for you?'

Bradman had already rehearsed this part of

the conversation.

'I think you will be aware, Mr Hampton, that we tend to work in the shadows. You would probably have decided for yourself that this job would probably be given to my department.'

'Well,' hedged the older man, 'I knew it would be removed from police jurisdiction. Beyond that, it was no concern of mine. Once they dropped the blanket over it, I'd no way of knowing whether it was being followed up, or quietly forgotten. As to your department, I didn't know there was such a thing. Is there?'

Wise eyes twinkled over the pipe. Bradman grinned.

'No, there isn't. It would appear in the Civil List if there was, wouldn't it? Public expenditure, and all that.'

'Exactly,' beamed Hampton. 'So, now that we've established that you don't exist, and cannot possibly be here, what is it you want?'

The percolator jumped, and the young man turned his head.

'Perfectly safe,' he was assured. 'One of the buttons it stands on is loose. I'm going to fix it tomorrow. You were saying?'

Bradman had lived alone long enough to know what tomorrow meant when it came to fixing things like coffee-pots.

'Well,' he began, 'when I was first told about this job, my reaction was that the police would do it much better. My boss agreed with me, but he pointed out that it wasn't possible, because far too many people would be involved, and total secrecy was the order of the day.'

The chief super nodded, without interrupting. It was a good start, he reflected. Obviously this young fellow did not see himself as some kind of hybrid between Sherlock Holmes and James Bond. Very good indeed.

'My trouble is,' continued Bradman, 'that I can't ask direct questions. Not as many as I'd like, anyway. I reach points where a bit of cross-examination would clarify things no end, but I can't use the technique. Not without arousing suspicion, not without making people wonder what could be so important about it all. Do you understand what I mean?'

'I think so, yes. You can't exactly say to anyone, can you prove where you were at such and such a time? That kind of thing.'

'That's it exactly. That's why I've come to you. If you would be good enough to bear with me, I'd like to tell you what I've been up to. It's possible that, with being so careful not to give anything away, I could have overlooked some perfectly simple area where I could ask questions without making people wonder why. And there's more to it than that. I know that you have personally been involved in many hundreds of murder investigations, and there is no substitute for that kind of experience. After you've heard me out, you may well be able to make a comment, which seems obvious to you but which I've overlooked.'

As he finished, he was wondering whether he had struck the right note. There was nothing on the grave face opposite to betray what was going on in his listener's mind.

He need not have worried. What had just been said was balm to the old policeman. It was not unlike having one of his whizz-kid inspectors coming to him with a problem.

'Before you start,' he enjoined gravely, 'are you sure that I ought to be hearing all this? Official Secrets Act, and all that? I mean, I am a signatory of course, but there are plenty of things I don't know about. Don't want to, either.'

The visitor had half-expected something of the kind, and was ready for it.

'I don't intend to embarrass you by giving you unnecessary information,' he assured his host. 'What I was proposing to do was to stick to the murder itself—oh yes, it's murder all right—and tell you what I know, and what I suspect. I don't see how that could cause you any difficulty. You were the first person in authority to have any knowledge of the circumstances, for one thing. For another, you have already been sworn to secrecy by your own Chief Constable. You are not only the ideal man for me to talk to, Mr Hampton. You are absolutely the only one to whom I can.'

It made sense, and put the pipe-smoker at his ease.

The percolator jumped again, and a red light switched on at the base.

'Coffee up,' he announced. 'I'll join you in a cup.'

Conversation was abandoned while he fussed around with mugs—'Don't bother with saucers these days'—and finally set the steaming beverage in front of his visitor.

'Been thinking about what you just said,' announced Hampton. 'On the whole, I don't suppose it can do any harm. As you pointed out, I have been told officially to forget the whole thing. You and your department don't exist, therefore you're not here. When you put those two things together, what do you have? One senior police officer, with an erased memory, sitting drinking coffee by himself. Nobody could take exception to that, I fancy?'

Bradman grinned.

'Then, since I'm not here, I'll just talk to myself for a while.' He sipped appreciatively at the strong coffee, and settled back in his chair. 'The facts are few, and very simple. The ramifications are almost infinite, so I'll leave them out of it for now. The facts, then. The deceased arrived home in mid-afternoon. There was nothing unusual about his behaviour or appearance. He changed his clothes and had a cup of tea. The housekeeper drank the same brew. He then spent the time until dinner alone in his study. There were no visitors to the house. Dinner was eaten at six-thirty, and it consisted of a strong curry. Mrs Cooper, that's the housekeeper, did not share the meal. She can't stand the stuff, and makes no bones about it. Sir Francis then went back to his study to work. The housekeeper went in at seven o'clock to ask if he wanted more coffee. He declined, but sounded perfectly normal. At seven-ten she went in again. She's quite adamant about the time, because she wanted to be free to watch television at seven-fifteen. Her employer was unconscious, if not already dead. She called for help at once. The doctor on stand-by, a man called Mellows, pronounced him dead. That was at eight-fourteen. He wasn't happy about the circumstances, but he kept his suspicions to himself, and then came to you. Those are the bare facts of the case, Chief Superintendent.'

Hampton nodded. He appreciated the way this young fellow had presented the case. Might have made a good police officer if he'd chosen that path. A least he hadn't dolled up the story with flights of fancy, or a lot of irrelevant material.

'I don't quite see why you have a problem,' he contributed. 'It's all quite clear, surely?'

Don Bradman thought he could detect something behind the words, but didn't know his man well enough to identify it.

'Not to me,' he admitted.

'Straightforward,' intoned Hampton. 'Mrs Cooper should be charged at once. Open and shut case. The man was all right when he got home. No one else spoke to him or came near him. She fed him herself, and was careful not to eat the same grub. Next thing we know, he's dead. She did it all right. No other possible explanation. Surprised at you, Don. I would have expected a probationer constable to have locked the woman up within the hour.'

The young man realised then that he was having his leg pulled. Unsmiling, he replied, 'I agree. And it would have been quite a long time before your constable's feet touched the ground, I imagine.'

'Ah. Why?'

'For any number of reasons. First and foremost, Mrs Cooper acted too quickly to be the guilty party. The moment she suspected something was wrong she sent for help.'

'That could have been to cover herself.'

Hampton was beginning to enjoy the conversation.

'Not if she wanted him dead,' repeated Bradman firmly. 'She would have left him for several hours, until it was bed-time, say. He would have been cold by then, and she could be certain. The medical people have made great strides in the last few years, thanks to our big drug problem. They can bring back people from the brink of death. They do it every day in every hospital, and they're getting better at it all the time. Mrs Cooper is an ordinary woman, with no medical training in her background. She had no way of knowing whether it would be possible to save Sir Francis when she picked up that telephone. If she had intended him to die, she would have waited.'

It made good sense, acknowledged the listener, but he wasn't going to let Bradman off too lightly.

'That sounds all right, as a piece of deductive reasoning from an intelligent person like yourself. But this lady, with all due respect to her, is only a simple person, as I understand it. She wouldn't have the benefit of your thought-processes.'

'No,' agreed Bradman. 'As you say, she is a simple, straightforward kind of person, and she thinks along those lines. She has a simple person's enormous faith in the ability of the doctors, and what they can do. She wouldn't have risked her employer's resuscitation by telephoning quite so quickly, not if she wanted him dead.'

'H'm.'

Hampton pretended to consider this in some depth. Then he said, 'You said there were other reasons. Could we talk about those?'

'There's motive. That's another big objection. They were strangers, these two. Met for the first time three months ago, when Sir Francis interviewed her for the housekeeper's job. Since then she hasn't seen him more than a dozen times. He only turns up at the house occasionally.'

The chief superintendent pointed his pipe.

'Three months can be a long time, between a man and a woman.'

The younger man half-smiled.

'Agreed, but I have the advantage of you there. I've seen this lady, spoken to her. She is not an attractive person, not in any way at all. Her appearance is downright homely, she is almost devoid of personality, and worst of all, has no trace of a sense of humour. I never met the late Mr Cooper, but I should think she was very fortunate ever to have been married at all. That may sound unkind, but it's no more than the truth.'

Hampton remained unimpressed on the surface.

'Anything else? What about his will? Perhaps he's left her the house, or something.'

'The house goes to his daughter, Melanie. Mrs Cooper has been left a sum of one hundred pounds for each year or part year she remains in his employ. Not exactly like winning the pools, is it?'

'The will must be new, then,' interjected Hampton. 'Since they did not know each other until recently.'

'Yes, it is. I don't know the exact date. Haven't seen it myself, but there should be a copy on its way to me. I'm very keen to see that document. It might point us in a whole new direction.'

'It might indeed,' agreed the chief superintendent. 'Still, let's stick to what we know for the moment. Is there any other reason for you to dismiss Mrs Cooper?'

Bradman heaved his shoulders.

'There is her transparent guilt,' he announced.

'Come again?'

'She is so obviously guilty, in every possible way. And where there is any doubt, anything which might suggest her innocence, or the involvement of a third party, she herself shuts off the likelihood.'

'Now then, Don, you're going to have to explain that rather more fully.'

Hampton leaned forward in his chair, all attention.

'She closes all the doors,' explained Bradman. 'I gave her every chance to suggest that someone else could have got into the house, without her knowledge. No way, she insists. The kitchen faces down the driveway, and it would be impossible for anyone to approach without her knowledge.'

'But what about the garden? She hasn't got all-round vision, I imagine?'

'No. But there again, she denies having left the kitchen at all. No one else had access to the food. She cooked it, she served it, and she watched him eat it. There was no third party.'

'Still, someone could have come through the

garden and got into the study that way, couldn't they?'

'Yes, they could. But it wouldn't have done them any good. She would have heard the voices. Mrs Cooper has most acute hearing, and she's very proud of it. If there'd been someone else in the study, she would have known. She's most insistent about it. Now, as to the poison itself. It's fast-acting, so the path people say. There was no way it could have been in Sir Francis' system for much more than half an hour without the effects beginning to show. He ate at six-thirty, and by ten past seven he was either dead, or on the brink of dying. Besides, if one even considers any other possibility but the evening meal, it means that someone in that study managed to get the dead man to take a fatal dose in those few minutes between his leaving the dining-room and Mrs Cooper calling in to ask about the coffee. It's all too absurd, and it won't hold water.'

Hampton's eyes twinkled.

'So it has to be Mrs Cooper. Right?'

'Right. And it isn't.'

Bradman's rejection was final. He looked at the older man, and widened his eyes.

'Now perhaps you can understand why I'm here.'

The policeman rested his pipe in the ash-tray, nodding.

'Thanks very much. What was it Roosevelt used to say, "The buck stops here"?'

‘It was Truman, actually,’ corrected his visitor. ‘And it isn’t your buck. It’s mine. Trouble is, I’ve nowhere to pass it.’

Hampton swallowed the last of his coffee.

‘Well, why not put it down for a moment? Let’s get away from your murder altogether. Let’s talk about murder in general. People tend to have a wrong conception of the word, you know. They start to think about deep plots, and country houses and all that paraphernalia. Seventy-five per cent of all murder, within the legal definition, is straightforward violence. Blunt instrument, knife, the occasional gun. Mostly committed by persons of low intelligence, on the spur of the moment, and frequently against virtual strangers. Premeditated murder forms a much smaller category, and doesn’t usually take very long to unravel, no matter what the novelists try to tell us. No matter how much trouble people go to, in order to prove they couldn’t have done it, the fact remains that nine times out of ten there isn’t any other candidate. It all comes down to why, you see. In order to want someone dead, you have to be very close to that someone, if their death is to bring any kind of satisfaction. The point is, what kind. Profit? Revenge? Jealousy, hatred, all the emotional stuff? It has to be someone very close, and that brings the candidates right down to a handful at most. In fact, the most usual situation is to find you are only dealing with two or three people, and it doesn't take long to work out which is guilty. And the more elaborate the scheme, the easier it is to take it apart, because there are far too many details to slot together. You can ask any policeman. Give him the choice between a closed-circle premeditated murder, and a hit-and-run killing on the highway, and he'll jump for the first one every time.'

Bradman was paying careful attention, but wondering where all this was leading.

'Poison, now, that's a rarity these days. Used to be quite popular years ago, but that was before the medical people improved their techniques. It's easy enough to get hold of the stuff, even feeding it to the victim, but you can't hope to fool the doctors. Not any more. Even so, it is still tried on occasions, and usually by women. Mixing it in with food is the most-favoured technique. There again, it means the culprit must have access to the food, and it doesn't take a genius to work out who did it. Now then, let's get back to your problem. You are saying you don't like Mrs Cooper for this job, and I understand your reasoning. Let's assume a third party, for the moment. How did he get the job done? That's the point. You must have thought about it.'

He looked expectantly at the serious face opposite, waiting.

'I appreciate what you've been saying, Mr Hampton, and indeed, I must admit I'd thought most of it through. I think what I've got here is the rarity. The really elaborate scheme. I've been thinking along those lines. The trouble is, my thoughts, such as they are, sound fanciful when you put them up against the kind of down-to-earth analysis you've just given.'

Hampton was careful to keep mockery out of his tone as he asked, 'What kind of thoughts? Blowpipes, poisoned darts, all that stuff?'

'It's been known,' insisted Bradman doggedly. 'After all, it's not so very long since that chap was stabbed with a poisoned umbrella-tip.'

The chief superintendent remembered the case. It was a political killing, which had caused quite a stir in the newspapers at the time.

'That's true,' he conceded. 'Well, go on.'

'I think I ought to be thinking more about the time Sir Francis was alone in that study. No matter what Mrs Cooper says, I'm sure that it would have been possible for someone to have got into the house without being seen. There are other ways to approach, without marching up the main driveway. Supposing it was someone Sir Francis was expecting, but didn't want Mrs Cooper to know about? It would have been simple enough for him to let them in, through a French door, and they could have left the same way.'

'But the poison,' objected the older man. 'What you're saying is that some unknown person was admitted secretly, by Sir Francis, stopped long enough to poison him, then slipped away again. How did he do it? Did he say "Just swallow this deadly draught, and I'll be off?" '

'There was a whisky decanter in the study. It was only part-full. Sir Francis might easily have had a drink, and this visitor could have added the poison to it.'

'M'm.'

It was thin, very thin. And the lack of conviction in the speaker's voice indicated how little faith he had in the idea.

'Well,' and Hampton tried to sound encouraging, 'it's not impossible, of course. Can't be ruled out. Better than the blowpipe, anyway.'

Bradman's gaze was quite steady as he replied, 'Matter of fact, that angle has been checked. I had the path people examine the corpse minutely for any signs of skin puncture. I was thinking mainly of hypodermic needles at the time, but it would cover your darts as well.'

'And they found nothing?'

'No recent marks whatever. The poison that killed Sir Francis Waterman could only have been administered by mouth. So, in a way, I'm back to square one.'

And to Mrs Cooper, thought Hampton, but he kept his thoughts to himself.

‘So you’ll be concentrating on your third party. Any ideas as to who it could have been?’

The visitor smiled ruefully.

‘Just between ourselves, the more I hear about the deceased the longer the list becomes. The number of people who aren’t sorry he’s dead seems to grow with every conversation I hold.’

The chief superintendent produced a battered tobacco-pouch, and began restuffing his pipe.

‘I can’t help you much there, I’m afraid. As you said, this is a one-man enquiry, and you are that one man. But I have one thought which I’m a bit nervous about mentioning.’

‘Please don’t be,’ begged Bradman. ‘I came here to listen.’

‘Very well. I can’t do anything official, naturally. But what I can do is to be a nosey copper. No one will think that’s unusual, least of all my own people. I was thinking of going into Mrs Cooper’s background a bit. Find out what she was doing as a young girl. Never know, she could turn out to have been one of Waterman’s birds, years ago. No harm in looking.’

And not much point either, thought Bradman privately. Still, he couldn’t turn down any offers.

‘I’d be grateful if you would,’ he said, with more enthusiasm than he felt. ‘She would make a lovely candidate, if only there were some connection.'

'Leave it with me,' Hampton told him heartily. 'I'll know more about that lady in twenty-four hours' time than her husband knew the whole time they were married. Anything else I can do for you?'

He'd quite taken to this young fellow. Not one of the supercilious sort, which you sometimes found with people who'd been promoted fast at a young age. Willing to listen, and to ask questions. Only way to learn, in Hampton's experience. This chap Bradman was going to amount to something, no doubt about that, and if he could help him on his way, he would do it.

'No, thank you, Chief Superintendent.' Bradman rose to go. 'It's done me good, talking to you. Helped to get my own mind clear. The inside of my head was getting a bit overgrown. I think I've rather a better idea of what I'm up to. Thanks again.'

They walked to the door, and the chief superintendent opened it.

'Give me a ring tomorrow night,' he suggested. 'If there's anything worth knowing about that lady, I should have it by then.'

'Fine. Well, good night.'

The man at the door stood watching as the visitor climbed into his car, waved, and drove away.

Well, reflected Hampton, sooner him than me.

CHAPTER NINE

When Bradman finally reached his flat, it was one-fifteen a.m. Summoned from his bed at six o'clock the previous morning, he had been on continuous duty for just over nineteen hours. Even so, the day's work was not yet ended. There was the business of the answering machine to be dealt with before he could contemplate any sleep.

In the small, immaculate kitchen, he made himself a mug of instant coffee, grateful for the familiar tang. Somebody had once told him he ought not to drink so much of the stuff. That was all very well, but no other solution was offered to the problem of staying alert for lengthy periods. Alcohol was reliable for a quick lift, but it soon wore off, and had to be replenished. At least, with coffee, a man didn't start dancing on tables and inviting everyone to join in the chorus.

Carrying his drink, he went and sat down by the low table where there reposed one telephone, one answering machine, one note-pad and pen. He was a man who prided himself on his memory, but never forgot what he had been told early in his career.

'You may think you have the finest memory in the world, and perhaps you have, but it's no match for a note-pad.'

He lit a cigarette, and switched on the machine. There were two messages. The first was a woman's voice, brisk and business-like.

'This is Aunt Alice. Please call me when you get home. Never mind what time it is. I shan't be able to sleep until you do.'

That meant they had some information for him at his base. There was always someone on duty at that particular number, which was changed every week. Before calling, he was curious to hear the second message.

This was from a different woman entirely. Veronica Broadhurst did not sound at all pleased.

'David, you know how I hate talking to this bloody machine. Where are you, anyway? Why don't you call me? He's only away for three days, and we've wasted one already. You've no right to treat me like this, job or no job. It's seven o'clock in the evening, and there's a whole night to get through. It's altogether too bad of you, and—'

There was more. Bradman sat, listening to the tirade, and wondering, not for the first time, what was to be done about Veronica. He had thought, at the outset, that she was just another wealthy, spoiled woman, who would use him as a diversion for a few weeks, and then drift naturally away. Months had gone by now, and there was no sign of a break. Yes, he decided, something would have to be done, something positive. But not tonight.

Relieved to have shelved the problem for the moment, he dialled 'Aunt Alice's' telephone number.

A receiver was lifted at the other end, and a voice said, 'Yes?'

'I'd like to speak to Aunt Alice, please.'

'Who wants her?'

'Tell her it's her favourite nephew, the cricketer.'

'Really? What's your average?'

'You'd have to ask Uncle.'

He always felt something of a fool going through this footling exchange, but they had to be careful. A new voice sounded in his ear.

'Don? This is the A. D.'

The Assistant Director himself no less, and at this hour. If Bradman had needed any reminder of the importance attached to his current assignment, the presence of such a luminary in the middle of the night would more than suffice.

'Hallo, sir,' he replied. 'Have you got something for me?'

'Yes. You put in a request for information about a girl named Maude Ryan.'

'Yes, I did. Any luck?'

'Quite a lot,' was the dry response. 'The girl came quite close to causing a major scandal some years ago, just as we were in the middle of some tricky Common Market talks. Your man was very prominent in the negotiations, and it would have been a nasty embarrassment if she hadn't been steered off.'

Steered off, reflected Bradman drily. There could be a wealth of meaning in that harmless-sounding phrase, but he knew better than to ask for details.

'What happened, after she was—um—diverted, sir?'

'She was pregnant, of course. Claimed your man was responsible. Still, there's a list of women as long as your arm who've made that claim. Couldn't prove anything.'

'Did she have the child?'

'Yes. A boy. It was back in nineteen seventy something. Let me see. Yes, here it is. He'd be eleven now. I'm still trying to find out where they are at present. I imagine you're still interested?'

'Extremely, sir,' he confirmed quickly. 'And thank you for what you've found so far.'

'Wait a minute, don't go away. There's some more stuff for you. A couple of dog-catchers went to call on a certain well-known gambling man.'

Dog-catchers. That was another departmental euphemism. What the A. D. meant was that a couple of strong-arm goons had been to scare the wits out of Alessandro Nicos.

'How did they get on?' queried Bradman.

'Oh, all right I think. He ranted and raved a bit. Usual sort of stuff about the Gestapo, the Russians have nothing on us, all that rubbish.'

'But is he going to be good?'

'Oh yes. I imagine so. He's under no illusions about what will happen if he isn't. He's either going to be very, very good, or very, very sorry. The man's not a fool, you know. I don't think the lady needs to worry about him.'

'Very relieved to hear it, sir.'

'And, speaking of the lady, she's been on to our export company, asking for you. Did you give her the number?'

Wondering whether he might be in for a dressing-down, Bradman said hastily, 'Had to give her something, sir. I've only got three numbers to choose from. There's my private number, which almost no one gets, in accordance with instructions. There's Aunt Alice, and I needn't say more about that. Then there's the export company. I could hardly tell the girl I had no telephone. Not in this day and age. What did she want, anyway?'

The A. D. considered what he'd been told, before replying.

'H'm. No harm done I suppose. It really is an export company, after all. Just don't get too free with it, that's my advice. Want? Oh, nothing. She just said it was a personal matter, and would they ask you to call her when you could.'

Ah. Personal, eh? The last thing Bradman needed just at that time was another Veronica Broadhurst.

'Thank you, sir,' he said, non-committally.

The A. D. was not prepared to leave the subject.

'Don, you call that girl. Can't have her pestering the export people. They might start to get nosey, and we really can't have that sort of thing. You deal with it. Call her off.'

'Right, sir, I'll deal with it tomorrow. Is that the lot?'

'That's all for now,' confirmed the Assistant Director. 'Where are you off to now?'

Bradman looked at his watch. It was one-forty a.m.

'I thought about going to bed for a couple of hours. I have to get a milk-train to Manchester at five-thirty.'

'I see. Well, be sure you don't miss it.'

There was a click, and that was all. No farewells, no good luck messages. Just a click. The department claimed to be impersonal, reflected Bradman sourly, and it certainly lived up to its claims.

Well, if he was to get any sleep at all that night, he'd better get to bed.

* * *

At nine o'clock the following morning he was ushered into a small third-floor room overlooking Manchester's Piccadilly. The bearded man who sat watching his entrance was the fearsome Professor Angus Fogg, hitherto no more than a name and a famous face to the newcomer.

'Bradman, isn't it?'

'Yes. How do you do, sir.'

'How do. Take a seat.'

The huge hand which Fogg extended was covered with the same aggressive black hair as his face. The eyes were almost black, too. Piercing, almost threatening, as they raked Bradman over.

'It's good of you to see me, Professor—' he began.

'Balls,' was the immediate response. 'It isn't good of me at all. You are here because Hugh Robertson blackmailed me, so don't let's fart about with protocol.'

Bradman was rather taken aback. When he had telephoned Robertson's office, seeking help with this interview, he had simply been told there would be no problem, and to report to Fogg's office at nine the next morning. Blackmail?

'I think you ought to explain that,' he suggested.

The black eyes flashed.

'Oh, you do, do you? All innocent, are we? Very well. These offices are on a monthly Government lease. We pay no rent, because we haven't any money. It's what you might call a goodwill gesture by the Government. My old and dear friend Hugh telephoned me. He said you wanted to see me urgently, and he hoped the offices were proving convenient. He also said he was sure there wouldn't be any problem with the monthly renewal, which is due in three days' time. That, sonny boy, is blackmail. What would you call it?'

Bradman shook his head.

'I had no idea,' he denied. 'I was simply told that you would see me, and I was grateful. I still am.'

'H'm.' Fogg breathed noisily, still studying the visitor. 'You're obviously some kind of whizz-kid, from some back-door Government agency. Oh, you need not bother either to deny or confirm. You'd probably tell me lies anyway. You want to talk about Waterman, I gather. Well, what about him?'

It was obvious there would be no point in dressing up the conversation. Plain words were clearly the order of the day.

'Sir Francis was active in many directions,' began Bradman. 'My job is to find out whether his death can be used in any way to discredit him, or the work he was doing.'

'Why?'

'Because there are always vultures around, waiting to feed from the dead. I am to forestall them, if I can.'

'You've a very direct way of speaking,' accused Fogg.

'It's the people one meets,' returned Bradman coldly.

A great hairy fist banged on the desk-top as

the professor gave one of his famous snorting laughs.

'We might get on. Yes, we might get on, despite your blackmailing buddies.' Then the good humour went from his face, as he rested on his elbows, and stared at the visitor. 'As to the vultures, I'll tell you this. If the carcase is half as rotten as the living man was, you'll never keep 'em off.'

Don Bradman managed to absorb this without shock. He was rapidly becoming accustomed to the professor's style.

'I'll have to ask you to elaborate,' he said, keeping his voice calm. 'It was my impression that you and Sir Francis were side by side in leading this movement.'

Fogg pulled back in his chair, hooding his eyes as he did when some television interviewer tried to catch him out.

'Was it? Was it really? How much do you know about the Campaign for Individual Liberty?'

'It's an attempt to gather under one umbrella all the small organisations which are concerned about the loss of people's rights. I couldn't begin to list all the groups involved, but I know it ranges from racial equality rights down to tenants' associations. The whole spectrum.'

'Not bad, not bad. What is happening is that small injustices are occurring right across the board. Sometimes these are the results of deliberate policy. Sometimes they are unintentional. The origin is unimportant. At the end of the day a few more people are a bit worse off than they should be, and another little protest group is formed. Nobody minds. They have no power, no funds as a rule. They get a little bit of publicity, and everyone thinks something is being done, so there's no need to get upset. The very existence of these tuppenny ha'penny outfits ensures that in fact nothing ever will get done. They are very often little more than pressure-valves. A place where people can get rid of their excess steam without any risk that something might get done. Can you recall the last time a government, any government, put through new legislation as a result of pressure from one of these organisations? Don't bother to scratch your head, because the answer is no. You can't, and neither can anyone else. That is why a few of us, from all political persuasions, decided that the only answer was to have one voice. A kind of national ombudsman, if you like. That is how the Campaign got its start.'

'I understand that, sir,' pointed out the visitor, 'but I also understood that Sir Francis was one of those few you mentioned. If you had such a poor opinion of him, how did that come about?'

Professor Fogg bared his huge teeth in a scowl.

'Ah yes. I'd have to blame myself for that.

You see, Mr Bradman, I'm no politician. Oh, I'm learning, fast, but I'm new to the game. You know my background, I expect? University, and so forth. Bit of an intellectual I suppose you could say. I had a growing awareness of the need for something like the Campaign, and I started talking to one or two people. When the celebrated Sir Francis Waterman showed an interest, I was delighted. This was the sort of support we needed. Man of the people, champion of the oppressed, and so forth. Ideal choice. Oh, yes, I was very unlearned in some ways.'

His voice tailed away, and he seemed to become preoccupied with his own thoughts.

'You found him a disappointment?' was the prompt.

'Huh,' snorted the beard. 'Understatement of the year. A ruthless, self-seeking bastard, was the unlamented Waterman. Used us. Used all of us, to further his own ends. And worse. He would use confidential information, which some of those splinter groups provided, in order to get people discredited. Prosecuted, even, in a couple of cases. Oh, he was a lovely man.'

'But surely,' objected the listener, 'once you found out that sort of thing was going on, you should have disassociated the Campaign from him?'

The professor sighed, and stared pityingly across the room.

'And I thought I knew little about politics. You, my friend, are even wetter behind the ears than I was two years ago, when all this started. Dissociate, you say? No chance of that. For one thing, I could never have proved anything against him. He was too fly for that. We all knew, of course, but that's a far cry from proof. And that wasn't the biggest handicap. Can you imagine the uproar, the public outcry, if the distinguished humanitarian should become separated from the Campaign? Who would suffer, eh? Answer me that. Who would suffer? The celebrated parliamentarian, the former minister, the man who was knighted for his good works? Or a bunch of scruffy intellectuals, with direct lines to Communist headquarters? The bleeding heart brigade. A lot of people would have loved to discredit us in precisely those terms right at the outset, but they didn't dare. Not as long as Sir Francis Waterman had a seat on the board. Do you see?'

Bradman could see very well. He could also see that the death of Sir Francis was in many ways an ideal solution from the point of view of Angus Fogg and his fellow-men. As to whether any of them would go as far as murder, he couldn't be sure, but there was another, richer source. There were the people who had suffered directly from his misuse of Campaign information. And, he reflected unhappily, it might be a very long list indeed.

One thing was certain. He would have to go elsewhere for that information. Professor Angus Fogg, for all his excellent qualities, could not be trusted with the truth about Waterman's death. Sooner or later his explosive personality would be unable to contain the facts, and the balloon would go up.

But there was one possible avenue which could be fruitful.

'I wonder whether I might be able to help,' he suggested. 'Is there any particular group of people who are about to be discredited, or even prosecuted, as a result of Sir Francis' activities here?'

Black eyes squinted at him.

'Why do you ask?'

'I have been given a certain amount of authority,' was the careful reply. 'Not unlimited, naturally, but a certain amount. It might just be possible to forestall any action which is being contemplated.'

It might also be possible to have a good look at the people concerned, to see whether any of them might have been driven to the extremity of murder, he thought privately.

Fogg was squirming around in his chair. It was a sure sign that he was undecided, although his audience had no way of knowing that.

'Do you seriously mean that you can interfere with the course of justice, if that's the appropriate word?'

'I would never suggest that,' came the disclaimer. 'But further consideration is sometimes given, in the light of new circumstances. It would not make good reading on Sir Francis' epitaph, that his last act was to persecute some harmless group of citizens. I think you take my point?'

'Yes I do,' the professor said emphatically. 'And I like it. Like the irony of it. We'd be doing the right thing, and for the wrong reason.'

Bradman lifted his eyebrows enquiringly.

'Well, don't you see, man?' explained Fogg tetchily. We'd be saving these poor sods, not because it's the right thing to do, but because it will ensure no mud gets thrown at the funeral of the bastard who started the trouble in the first place. We would be protecting his good name. Blast his black soul.'

'If I could have the details, then?'

It wasn't a very promising situation, he realised, as he made a note of what the professor told him. There was a housing dispute, involving the local Asian community, and it developed that there were some illegal immigrants among the complainants. This was to be used to undermine the main points under contest, and could well be a decisive factor. It all seemed a far cry from an unexplained death in Surrey, particularly since the locale was in Birmingham, but it would have to be followed up.

‘I make no promises, Professor Fogg, but I’ll certainly have this looked at.’

‘I believe you will,’ said the professor, rising to see him out. ‘I believe you will. Be a great joke, wouldn’t it, if some good were to come out of that gentleman’s demise?’

‘It would have to be a very private joke,’ Bradman reminded. ‘Only you and I will ever know it.’

A great roar of laughter followed him down the corridor.

CHAPTER TEN

The air had been quite chilly when Bradman left his flat in the grey dawn, and he had dressed appropriately. As the morning wore on, there had been a sudden shift in the weather, and a most unseasonal outburst of warm sunshine. By the time he returned to London he was thoroughly uncomfortable, and realised he would have to divert back to the flat in order to find more suitable clothing.

There was some post on the floor of the tiny hall, and he picked it up on his way through. A well-known travel company was proud to announce slashing reductions on its return flights to Sri Lanka, someone else was delighted to be able to offer him special membership terms for a nearby massage parlour, and the bank were kindly drawing his attention to a certain overdraft, which he would doubtless be clearing in the near future. He dropped those items on the nearest table and opened a familiar grey envelope from the department.

Inside was a single typed sheet, confirming the information the A. D. had given him over the telephone about Maude Adams. Her name did not appear, and to a casual reader the report would have been merely a rather boring list of dates and places. There was no heading, and no indication of the addressee. Bradman thought the department overdid it sometimes, with this slavish devotion to anonymity. He scanned the paper quickly, but except that there was more detail, there was no salient point which the A. D. had not covered the previous evening. There wouldn't be, of course.

While he was stripping off, he switched on the answering machine, turning up the volume.

Veronica had been on again, with a brand new outburst. It wasn't hard to deduce that she had drunk herself to sleep the night before, overslept, and woken up with a nasty hangover, which she promptly proceeded to vent over the telephone. Women, he decided, could be the very devil when a man had his work to do. Let's see, this was the second day of her husband's absence. If he didn't do something to calm her down before her lord and master came home there was no predicting what she might do. One thing was certain, risky or not, he could not leave this present job on Veronica's account, no matter what trouble she might stir up for him later. He'd have to think up something.

And, on the subject of women, he ought to telephone Melanie Nicos. He couldn't have her pestering the export company again, not after the A. D. had warned him once.

After a quick shower, he put on a cotton shirt and lightweight trousers, and felt like a new man. With a cup of coffee and a biscuit by way of lunch, he lit a cigarette and dialled the number Melanie had given him. The ringing lasted for several seconds, and he was just about to hang up when the receiver at the other end was lifted.

'Hallo? Hang on a minute, will you?'

He hung on, puzzled. Then the voice came back.

'Sorry about that. I had to rush up the stairs when I heard the phone, and then I was too out of breath to talk. Who is it?'

'Don Bradman, the non-cricketer,' he replied.

'Oh, Don, I'm so glad it's you. Listen, what did you do to Alex?'

'I didn't do anything to him,' he denied quickly. 'Why, what's up?'

She chuckled, a warm rich sound.

'Oh, nothing's up. Everything is absolutely splendid. He rang me up. Said he was so sorry to hear about my father, and to tell me I had nothing to worry about from him. Let bygones be bygones, that was what he said, especially at a time of bereavement. Honestly, he was such a hypocrite, I could have been sick. Now, he's sent flowers. Millions of 'em. They're hanging off the lampshades. You must have put the fear of God into him. I can't tell you how grateful I am.'

Well, well, thought the object of all the gratitude. This was a situation that might be turned to some profit, if it weren't for the background presence of Veronica Broadhurst.

'I'm very glad it's worked out to your satisfaction,' he said unctuously. 'I'd steer clear of that gentleman though, just the same, if I may suggest it. I think he's bad news.'

The reaction was immediate. 'You don't have to tell me anything about that one, thank you. I've been there. Now then, I think there's something I can do for you. Are you free at the moment?'

Bradman had no doubt of that, although he would have preferred to raise the subject himself.

'Well,' he hesitated, 'as a matter of fact—'

'It could be important,' she interjected. 'You're still chasing round after Daddy's papers, aren't you?'

'Why yes,' he replied, surprised at what he thought was a change of subject.

'Well, I've got something that might interest you. Have you ever heard of a man named Kennedy? James Austin Kennedy?'

Kennedy, Kennedy. Bradman racked his brain.

'I don't think so,' he admitted finally. 'Not just off-hand. What about him?'

'That's just it. I don't know. Look, let me explain.'

'Oh please. Yes.'

There was a short pause before Melanie resumed.

'Now look, Don, I don't think you're going to like this. You'll probably tick me off, or something.'

Oh Lord, he reflected, wondering what was to come.

'I can't really judge that until I know what it is,' he pointed out reasonably.

'M'm.' She still sounded hesitant. 'Look, I'd sooner deal with this face to face. Could you come round here? Now, I mean.'

Bradman looked at his watch. It was almost two-fifteen. There was no actual appointment which would prevent him from going to see her. On top of which, it sounded as though she could have some information of value.

'You're sure we can't cover it over the phone?' he queried.

'No,' was the emphatic response. 'No, I really think you ought to come. You have the address, haven't you?'

'Yes.' In fact, Melanie Nicos lived in an expensive block of flats not ten minutes away from his own place.

'How long will it take you to get here?'

'Let's see.' He didn't want her to know how close he lived. Then he realised she had no way of knowing he was calling from home. 'Matter of fact I'm in a friend's office at the moment, not all that far from you. I could probably be there in ten or fifteen minutes.'

They ended the conversation, and Bradman sat, staring thoughtfully at the wall. He could put a call through to Aunt Alice, get the preliminary feelers out on this Kennedy. On the other hand, if he left it until he'd heard what Melanie had to say, he might be able to save Auntie some time. A few minutes later, he left the flat and walked round to keep the appointment.

He was not left to cool his heels at the apartment door. His finger had hardly touched the buzzer before the door opened, and she stood looking at him.

'That was quick,' he acknowledged, moving inside.

'I can be quick about things, once I've made up my mind,' was the mysterious reply.

The place was much as he would have envisaged it, knowing the occupant and the price range. Softly luxurious would sum it up very nicely, he decided, and tasteful into the bargain. Mind you, it wasn't easy to judge, with vast flower displays spilling from every surface. The air was heady.

'I would have brought some flowers,' he told her, grinning, 'but the shop was empty. Now I see why.'

'Huh,' she retorted. 'I'm going to get someone from the hospital to come and cart them away. Can I get you a drink?'

'No thanks, it's too hot. You go ahead, if you want to.

He didn't want to get into any situation of an intimate kind with this particular lady. The situation was precarious enough already, what with the warmth and the sense-stirring perfume of the massed flowers. Melanie Nicos was wearing a thin yellow sun-dress, which did a great deal for her tanned arms and shoulders, but contributed nothing to Bradman's ease of mind.

'Well, do sit down at least. Perhaps we can have a drink later.'

Later? What did she mean, later? What did she imagine was going to be happening in the meantime? He selected a chair which was isolated from the rest of the furniture, and perched dutifully on the edge.

His hostess watched the performance with an amused glint in her eye. He was going to take a lot of trouble to keep things formal, this attractive man with the mysterious powers to get things done. Well, perhaps it was just as well, for the moment. Much would depend on how cross he was going to be with her during the next few minutes. Afterwards—well, we'd see. Following his example, she sat down on another upright chair, smoothing at the dress so that at least her bare knees were covered. That ought to satisfy him.

'I hope you're not going to be too angry with me. The fact is, I kept something from you yesterday.'

He looked at her patiently, and waited. Seeing that he wasn't going to react, she continued.

'Yes, it was while I was going through Daddy's things. I'd thought the chances were that anything he was holding about Alex would be locked up. There were some keys. I put them in my bag. That was before you arrived, of course. I took them with me when I left.'

Bradman tried to stem his rising annoyance. Keeping his voice calm, he put a question.

'But I thought we understood each other, after our talk? I thought you trusted me?'

She shook her head slightly, and a sweep of gleaming black hair fell across one cheek. Brushing it aside she replied, 'No. Not altogether. I wanted to trust you, wanted to believe you could do what you said. But that isn't the same thing as knowing.'

He acknowledged this with a nod.

'I see. And now you know, is that it?'

She waved a hand towards the riot of flowers.

'The proof is all round me.'

'What about these keys, then?'

Melanie picked at the hem of her dress.

'There was one person I was sure Daddy would have trusted, and that was the whore, Angela I mean, just for definition. He probably had others, but she was closer to him than anyone. Certainly than any of his family,' she added bitterly. 'If he had some papers he wanted no one else to know about, I thought he might keep them at her place. So, I went round to see her. She wasn't in. In fact, by the look of the place she's cleared off somewhere.'

By the look of the place? Despite all his training, Bradman knew he could never surmise such a thing from looking at the outside of a building.

'You went inside, then?' he accused. 'One of the keys fitted.'

She lowered her eyes.

'Yes,' she admitted. 'It seemed like a golden opportunity, and the way I was feeling I didn't give a damn whether she came back and caught me. Yes, I went in, and I'd do it again.'

He had no wish to interrupt the flow by moralising at this stage, so he said simply, 'I see. Please go on.'

Relieved that he had not yet taken her to task, Melanie resumed.

'Miss Dunning,' and she emphasised each syllable with clear distaste, 'whatever else she may be, is a fastidious person. But the flat was in a mess, rather. It looked to me as though she'd packed her bag and left in a hurry. Anticipating the reporters, I expect. Or someone like you.'

She looked at him for some reaction.

'Possibly,' he conceded. 'I don't yet see where this man Kennedy comes in.'

'Ah. Well, I decided it was too good an opportunity to miss. When I went to the place it was really to ask Angela if she had any papers of Daddy's. With her out of the way I could look for myself. I found a tin box. It was inside a shoe-box actually, on top of the wardrobe. Not exactly what you'd call top security. It was locked, but I found a small key on the ring which opened it.' She stared straight into Bradman's face. 'I realised at once what I'd found. And what you were after. You're not some kind of high official at all, are you? You're a spy, like Daddy was.'

It needed all the calm the seated man could muster to control his facial muscles.

'I'm sorry, Melanie, but you're talking completely over my head,' he assured her. 'This is the most arrant nonsense. What makes you say such a thing?'

There was excitement building up inside him, that feeling which is unique to the trained investigator, that something is at last about to become clear.

Melanie was disappointed at his calm reaction. There ought to have been something more dramatic from him, she felt. Getting up suddenly from her chair, she pulled open a drawer in the telephone-table and pulled out some documents. Striding across the room, she thrust them into Bradman's hands.

'There's the proof,' she announced theatrically. 'Try talking your way out of those.'

Carefully, the puzzled Bradman opened the first document, with its familiar thick paper. It was a birth certificate for one James Kennedy Austin.

'Look at the date of birth,' she invited. 'same year as Daddy.'

True enough, the year was 1921. He turned next to the worn passport. That too was in the name of Austin, but the photograph inside was that of Sir Francis Waterman, wearing an uncharacteristic moustache. The visa papers were stamped repeatedly over a period of the preceding three years. The languages were alternately Spanish and Portuguese, but the entry points were all in South America. There were other papers, too. Photostats of letters of credit, all Spanish now.

'Well,' demanded the waiting girl.

'This is all new to me,' he confessed. 'I really don't know what to make of it. Tell me, do you speak any Spanish? I was just wondering if you could explain these things?'

He indicated the letters of credit.

'Not a word,' she said. 'But they're obviously business papers of some kind. Anyway, that's beside the point. My father has been nipping over to these places when he's supposed to have been on holiday abroad, or on some trade mission in China or somewhere. You people must have known all about it. Who else could give him a proper passport and everything? Well, come on, Don, admit it. I've really stumbled on something, haven't I?'

The answer to her question was an unequivocal 'yes'. The point at issue was to know what any of it meant. Bradman picked his words with care.

'Melanie, you are asking me to be honest with you, and that's what I'm going to be. This stuff is a complete mystery to me. I haven't the foggiest idea what any of it means, and that is the absolute truth. On the face of it, I think you might be right. This alternative identity business could mean that your father was carrying out some undercover work for one of our hush-hush departments. I wouldn't know anything about that side of things, and I have no wish to know. However,' he continued hastily, seeing that she was about to interrupt, 'I have one advantage. I do know where to go and ask questions.'

'Ah,' she breathed. 'You're not coming the complete innocent with me, then. That's something, I suppose.'

'I am not coming anything with you at all,' he assured her, rising to his feet. 'As I say, I have no first-hand knowledge of what you call this spy business, but I do know where to ask. And the sooner I get on with it, the better. Was there anything else in the box?'

'Only this.'

She held up a small flat key. On the side was a serial number.

'You'd better give it to me.'

He put the documents and the key into his pocket. Then he stood before her, and his eyes were grave.

'I think you may have become involved in

something quite outside your comprehension, or mine. For pity's sake say nothing of this to anyone. Not to anyone, you understand?'

There was no misunderstanding the seriousness of his words. She felt suddenly rather isolated and helpless.

'I wouldn't, naturally. But it couldn't do any harm, could it? I mean, Father is dead, after all.'

Bradman shook his head.

'That is beside the point. We don't know what he was doing, or for whom. One thing is certain, there's something big involved here. Whatever it is will continue, whether your father's part in it comes to an end or not. These people operate at a very delicate level. They take no chances, can't afford to, with the issues involved. If they thought you might upset things, I couldn't be responsible for your safety. You understand what I'm saying?'

Her eyes were frightened now, and he was relieved to see it.

'It's too bizarre,' she protested. 'Are you saying that our own people would harm me? Bit far-fetched, isn't it?'

'No,' he rejected flatly. 'Big issues cannot be set aside simply to accommodate one individual. The machine rolls on. The thing is, not to get in its path. Take my advice, Melanie, put all this completely from your mind. It's the only way, believe me.'

She bit at her lip, convinced finally.

‘Will you tell me what happens?’

‘If I’m allowed to,’ he said simply. ‘Otherwise, no.’

‘That’s honest, at least.’ Then she brightened ‘Well, I should think this calls for a drink now, wouldn’t you?’

He shook his head, regretfully.

‘More than I dare,’ he replied. ‘The stuff you’ve found is dynamite, believe me. I have to get rid of it as fast as I possibly can. Next time, eh?’

She put a hand on his lapel and looked up into his face.

‘Will there be a next time?’

What kind of job is this, he reflected, when I have to walk out on such a woman?

‘Oh yes,’ he assured her, and meant it. ‘There’ll be a next time.’

CHAPTER ELEVEN

Aunt Alice had not been at all pleased with Bradman's urgent demand to see Sir Edward. There was protocol to be observed, procedures to be followed. Perhaps if he could give some inkling of the need for haste—but he remained firm. As he had so often found in the past, he could not make up his mind as to whether the obstacles put in his way were really as necessary as people made them sound. He sometimes thought there was another element involved, the perfectly human desire to know what was going on, and an inbuilt resistance to being excluded. Even inside the department, he had found, people were not above petty jealousies at times.

Still, he had remained adamant, and was told curtly to call again in thirty minutes. The second call had proved more fruitful, and he had been told, in tones of icy detachment, what he must do next.

It was almost five o'clock that afternoon when he walked into the dusty little newsagent's shop again. The door had been wedged open, to allow in any fresh air that might have survived the baking pavements outside. The interior of the place was musty and stale. There were no other customers this time, and the shopkeeper was leaning on the counter, reading one of his own evening papers.

There was no recognition on his face when he inspected the new arrival.

'From the V.A.T.,' explained Bradman.

'Thought you'd finished,' grumbled the owner.

'Just a couple of points,' smiled Bradman. 'Shouldn't take long.'

'H'm. Well, you know where everything is. The missus'll look after you. Tell her, if she's putting the kettle on, not to forget me.'

'I will.'

Five minutes later, as he sat outside the door of the room where he had originally been interviewed, it opened suddenly, and Sir Edward stood, beckoning him inside.

'I trust you will be able to justify this most unusual course,' was the greeting.

'I think so, sir.' I've come across something most unusual.'

Leaning over the desk, Bradman carefully placed the documents in front of his waiting chief. Sir Edward stared at him very hard, before turning his attention to the papers. Then he read them, each in turn, and slowly.

'How did you come by these?'

Bradman recounted the story, exactly as Melanie Nicos had told it to him. There was no sign of any reaction from his chief.

'Mrs Nicos seems to have been one step ahead of you, then. How fortunate that she should choose to confide in you. Otherwise, this stuff may not have come to light for months. If ever.'

Sir Edward's tone was not friendly at all. Bradman had not known what reaction to expect, but he certainly hadn't anticipated a telling-off.

'As you say, sir, it's a stroke of luck.'

'What does the young woman make of it?'

Glad of the change of subject, Bradman replied, 'She thinks it means her father was engaged in some top-level diplomatic cloak-and-dagger work, sir. The word 'spy' was used.'

'Good grief.'

Sir Edward Houston was not of the breed of men who roll their eyes, but his intonation carried the same effect.

'And you, Bradman? What is your deduction?'

'Well, sir, if one discounts the theory that his daughter puts forward, there is only one explanation, as I see it. Sir Francis has been laying plans to do a bunk. Alternative identity, funds in foreign parts, where, incidentally, we have no extradition agreement.'

'Oh, you've checked that, have you?'

It was a catch question, and the denial was instant.

'Certainly not, sir. It's part of my tool-kit-I'm supposed to keep up-to-date on all questions of extradition.'

'H'm. You said just now 'if we discount Mrs Nicos' theory.' Have you any doubt?'

'My mind is completely open, sir. Sir Francis would have been an ideal man to undertake a delicate mission. It certainly would be no surprise to me if that were the case.'

The eyes across the desk were frosty. 'I see. And then Sir Francis, just to show how security-minded he is, ties up all the incriminating documents with a piece of pink ribbon and leaves them under his girl friend's pillow. Is that how you see it?'

The discomfited operative stuck to his guns.

'Stranger things have happened, sir,' he said doggedly. 'Only two years ago there were certain papers actually left in a taxi.'

It was an impudent reminder. The national outcry which followed that particular idiocy had reverberated throughout the department. Not the least of the developments which followed had been the removal of the director, and his replacement by one Sir Edward Houston. That worthy absorbed this latest remark carefully.

'You might find it profitable to do tongue-holding exercises each night, before retiring,' he advised finally. 'Let's talk about the other half of your theory. You think the woman is in on it? Angela Dunning?'

'Hard to say, sir, but I doubt it. She's pushed off, at the moment, I understand. Can't see her leaving this stuff lying about, if she had any idea what it was. Do we know where she is?'

'Naples,' was the rejoinder. 'She has a married sister there. I haven't thought it necessary to bring her back. This could change that, of course. You've read these letters. Is your Spanish up to it?'

'Oh yes, sir. James Kennedy Austin has the better part of two hundred thousand pounds waiting for him. The point is, where did he get it?'

'Where indeed?' mused Sir Edward. 'However, that's my province, not yours. Leave this stuff with me. I shall have to shift a bit, since there's no telling when Waterman intended to make his move. There may be things already in motion, and more especially so now that the principal is dead. What about that, by the way, any developments?'

'I've a lot of feelers out, sir. Aunt Alice ought to have some more information for me by tonight. I'm due to call in at ten o'clock.'

'Ten, eh?' Sir Edward thought for a moment. 'I'm changing your orders, as of now. Drop out of sight, leave everything. There's only you and the girl who know about this?'

He tapped at the documents.

'Yes, sir. Unless Miss Dunning—'

'Forget Miss Dunning. My concern is what's happening here, not in Italy. The girl is a risk. Keep her occupied until the ten o'clock call. I may have something for you by then.'

'Occupied, sir?'

'Incommunicado,' he was told firmly. 'Shouldn't be too hard to do. I've seen the young woman, remember. I can visualise worse assignments. Off you go.'

As Bradman left the shop, his thoughts were grim. The prospect of spending the next few hours with Melanie Nicos had its pleasing side, but it wasn't that that he was worried about. Sir Edward had said she was a risk, and that may have 'something' for him by ten o'clock. If it had been decided by then that Melanie was too much of a risk, Bradman was under no illusions about what the 'something' might be. It would be up to him to eliminate the risk, and there would be no discussion permitted.

He pulled up at the first telephone box he saw, and telephoned her to say he was on his way. She sounded quite pleased, almost gay, and her misunderstanding of his motives did nothing to lighten her spirits. The early evening traffic delayed him, and it took him almost half an hour to complete his journey.

Melanie was all smiles when she answered the door.

'When you said there would be a next time, I'd no idea you meant quite so soon. Did you find out anything, or aren't you allowed to say?'

Bradman pulled himself together. If this lovely creature was about to enter the 'file closed' category, the least he could do was to see that she enjoyed her evening. He followed her inside.

'They never tell me anything,' he assured her. 'It gave them something to think about, though. In fact, they gave me the evening off. I have to call in at ten o'clock, but until then, I'm on my own.'

Melanie wagged a reproving finger.

'Shame on you,' she mocked. 'You're the first man who ever called me invisible.'

'Oh, I didn't mean—'

'Too late,' she told him. 'I quite understand. You wish to spend the evening sitting in a dark corner by yourself. Just pretend I'm not here. Shouldn't be too difficult, since you can't see me. I'll just go on knitting a shawl, or something. Shan't disturb you.'

As she was about to move away, he put a restraining hand on her arm.

'Bit late for that,' he told her softly. 'I don't recall when I was more thoroughly disturbed.'

'Can't have that,' she murmured. 'Perhaps if you were to lie down for a while?'

He stroked at the shining black hair.

'Good idea. But I have this fear of being alone.'

'I could come, too. In case you needed anything.'

'Something does come to mind,' he admitted.

* * *

The doorbell was loud and insistent, and accompanied by someone banging at the panels.

'Someone at the door,' Melanie grumbled into his shoulder.

'Evidently,' he muttered. 'What are you going to do? It isn't my door.'

She raised her head, and grinned down at him from drowsy eyes.

'Lazy devil. I'll have to go. They'll have that door down in a minute. Be as quick as I can.'

Scrambling out of bed, she wrapped a dressing-gown around herself, and gave her hair a quick pat in the mirror.

'I look like the wrath of God,' she said contentedly. 'Thanks to you.'

'All thanks are entirely mine,' he assured her. 'If you'd care to hurry back, I'd like to thank you again.'

She gave him a slow smile, and went out, closing the door firmly behind her. The flat dated back to the days when privacy was still a factor, and the two-inch thick door acted as a seal against any noise coming in or out. Bradman reached for a cigarette, wondering idly who the caller might be. Not that it mattered a great deal. Whoever it was, they would get short shrift from Melanie, the mood she was in. There are times for people to call, there are other times. He yawned, and stretched himself against the crumpled pillows. This was one of the other times. Turning his back on the door, he was positioning an ash-tray when it opened.

'That took you long enough,' he grumbled.

'Sorry, we made it as fast as we could.'

The sound of a male voice made him turn sharply, sleep draining away as if by magic.

A tall, broad-shouldered man stood framed in the doorway, grinning down at him.

'Who the devil are you? Where's Mrs Nicos?'

'I'm Pritchard, Special Branch,' was the reply, and a familiar card was held out for him to inspect. 'We've had to take the young lady away, I'm afraid. It's Mr Bradman, isn't it?'

Take her away? Sir Edward's words came flooding back into his mind. 'Something' was being done about her. But it couldn't be that other thing, the something he had tried to put out of his mind. They wouldn't use Special Branch for that sort of work. It could still be very nasty, but it wouldn't be—that. A great relief flooded through him.

'Yes, I'm Bradman,' he agreed. 'Why've you taken her away? What is she supposed to have done?'

'Nothing, as far as we know. Our job is to put the fear of God into her. Make her suffer for a few hours, then get her to sign the Official Secrets Act. It seems the young lady has stumbled across certain information which could lead to a breach of the security regulations. If it got into the wrong hands, that is.'

'But you didn't even let her pack a bag.'

'All part of the psychology,' was the smooth reply. 'Instant cut-off from all familiar things. Makes people very receptive. Still, I'm not telling you anything you don't know, Mr Bradman.'

No, he wasn't. Bradman had recovered all his faculties now. In fact, he was feeling rather at a disadvantage, lying naked in bed, while this large, competent man stood there, speaking as though nothing unusual was happening.

'What will you tell her about me?' he demanded.

'I am to leave that to you,' he was told. 'We can play it any way you choose. We could tell her, if you like, that you arranged the whole thing. Or, we could say that you're playing hell, and that it's largely due to your intervention that we're letting her go so quickly. Up to you.' Pritchard looked around at the softly lit bedroom. 'It all comes down to whether you might need her future—um—co-operation, I suppose.'

Bradman glanced at him sharply, but the Special Branch man's face remained impassive. This was all a bit sudden. He would have liked a little more time to think about it. All very well for this chap Pritchard to present him with two clear alternatives. It wasn't his decision, after all. It wasn't Pritchard who stood to go down in Melanie's memory-book as the number one despicable character of all time. It wasn't easy at all. This had all the hallmarks of a most promising relationship. Melanie Nicos was a vital, intelligent woman, vibrantly attractive. On top of which, she felt herself to be in his debt, and really, it was asking too much of a man to expect him to throw all that away.

Blast Pritchard, blast the whole damned department.

Savagely, he ground out the last of his cigarette. The man in the doorway watched him.

'What's the answer, Mr Bradman?'

Pritchard had no doubt what his own answer would be. A man would have to be mentally deficient to throw away a set-up like this, and with that superb woman his men had just taken away.

The man on the bed stared at him with expressionless eyes, and when he spoke, the words sounded almost metallic.

'Tell her I set it up. You're simply carrying out my instructions.'

CHAPTER TWELVE

Precisely at ten that evening he called his Aunt Alice, and went through the usual preamble. Then, the voice at the other end said,

'Well, well, you seem to have stirred up quite a concoction. Thanks to you, this place has been staffed entirely with blue-assed flies all evening.'

The words were delivered with some asperity, and Bradman could not suppress a grin as he visualised the hive of activity he had set in motion.

'Sorry about that,' he offered. 'Anything for me?'

'The Great White wants to talk to you personally. He's just gone off to the inner room. Hold the receiver away from your ear.'

Bradman did so, and quickly. He had made the mistake once of being slow about it, and the resultant attack on his eardrums had caused him considerable discomfort for almost two days. In spite of all the security precautions about the Aunt Alice number, the department took no chance that it might fall into the wrong hands. With all the sophisticated monitoring techniques now available, there was only one way in which to be certain that illegal phone-tapping could be neutralised. The sudden introduction of a high-frequency signal from the receiving instrument would effectively damage any illicit reception for several minutes. Some boffin had attempted to explain the technicalities to him once, but Bradman was no scientist, and the lecture had gone over his head. The subsequent experience with the signal itself had not followed the same path. It had gone straight through his head, and left him a sadder man for almost forty-eight hours.

Counting off the prescribed eight seconds, he put the telephone gingerly back to his ear. There was silence.

'Bradman here, sir.'

'Ah yes,' came Sir Edward's urbane tones. 'Things don't seem to have worked out too badly. I haven't all the details yet, of course. It will take days, or possibly even weeks, before all the ramifications are known to us. The main issue, however, is all too regrettably clear. Our late, and wholly lamented friend had been making his own retirement provisions. For the past several months he has been setting up the most intricate arms deal with a certain small power. The initial delivery has already been made, and there's not much to be done about that. But the quantity was small, and enough for nuisance value only in the particular area concerned. A second shipment is already in transit, but our French friends have managed to impound it at Marseilles. I must say, they were sharp off the mark, our colleagues in Paris. Nice piece of international co-operation. It was a lucky thing for us that the man responsible happened to die when he did. Another month, and the whole business would have been completed. We've been lucky, Bradman, very lucky.'

'It might have worked out differently sir, but for the girl.'

Bradman was anxious that Melanie's part should not be overlooked. Despite the assurances from the Special Branch man, he felt uneasy about the department's intentions in that direction.

'Girl? What girl?'

The trouble with Sir Edward was, you could never be certain whether he was being playful.

'The daughter, sir. Some friends of ours asked her out this evening.'

'Ah yes, the daughter. The daughter, of course. Quite harmless, I have no doubt. Done us very well, in fact.'

'She'll be released then, without any difficulties?'

He didn't want to dwell too long on the implications of what 'difficulties' might mean.

'Don't see why not. She must be made to understand the situation, of course. Can't afford to have her running about talking to people. We shall spin her a yarn. Father engaged in work of vital secrecy, that kind of stuff. Should be all right, I fancy. Nothing for you to worry about.'

'Thank you, sir. Do I just carry on then, as before? With my assignment?'

'Oh, that. Well, look here, I really don't think we can waste much more time on it. We're not policemen, you know, and there's a whole pile of other stuff waiting.'

The listening man frowned. He was being given precisely the argument he had himself raised at the outset.

'Am I to pack it in then, sir? There are one or two promising enquiries going on.'

His master heard this impassively. Trouble with the younger chaps, they always got enthusiastic. Couldn't always see the larger issues. Well, it would do no harm to humour him, for a little while.

'You're obviously keen on this,' he said slowly. 'Tell you what, I can let you have another twenty-four hours, but that's the absolute limit. Can't have expensive people like you plodding around, playing Hawkshaw. Be extra careful, though, and remember what I've just told you. You're dealing with a public benefactor.'

'I'll remember. And thank you for the extra time.'

'Use it well. Might be interesting to know who saved the government all this embarrassment. That's all from me. I think the people here have some stuff you wanted. I'll hand you over.'

He was gone. Typical, reflected Bradman.

Typical of Sir Edward, typical of the whole bloody department. Terse, matter of fact, off-hand. Never mind the fact that they were dealing with big issues. Never mind that people's lives were involved. Never mind—

'Don?'

A new voice came on.

'I'm still here,' he confirmed.

'You were after whatever we could dig up about a woman called Maude Ryan. Bit of a dead end, I'm afraid. There's a mass of stuff here. Do you want to hear it all?'

'Yes, please. All of it.'

* * *

The next morning was bright and sunny, and the Guildford road as busy as ever. Preoccupied with his own thoughts, Bradman found himself in the wrong traffic lane, and was soon caught up in the traffic snarl of the city centre. In consequence, he had to head out on the Brighton road before he could make a U-turn and pick his careful way back to the side-road he needed. The end result was that he was twenty minutes later than he had planned in arriving at the tiny village where Sir Francis Waterman had met his death. He had studied the place on his last visit—was that only two days ago?—but that had only been from habit. He was glad of that habit now, as he drove into the narrow little main street.

There was only one place to park a car, and that was outside the church. He climbed out, locking up carefully. That too was habit, he reflected, with amusement. The number of car-thieves in a sleepy backwater like this would not be very large.

There were two shops. One was the combination newsagent, tobacconist, confectioners and post-office, complete with genuine Queen Victoria letter-box outside. The other was a curious hybrid of grocer-cum-supermarket, with windows almost obscured by brightly coloured 'Special Offer' stickers, many of them out of date.

Bradman walked slowly along the narrow pavement, conscious of the occasional scrutiny always made of obvious strangers in such communities.

The door of the grocer's was wedged open, and he went in, to find half-a-dozen customers wandering around, inspecting the packed shelves. There were two staff on view, a plump motherly-looking woman, faintly ridiculous in a pink overall and frilly mob-cap, and a man. The man was in his early sixties, with a tendency to stoop. Iron-grey hair surmounted a long, good-humoured face, with time-marks etched deeply.

Bradman made his way up to the cash-desk, where the man was busy emptying small bags of coins into the till.

'Mr Reynolds?'

The man looked up.

'Yes. Good morning.'

'Could I see you for a moment? Offices, Shops and Railway Premises Act. I'm from the Town Hall. The name is Bradman.'

Reynolds inspected him, nodding.

'Shan't be a minute. Just finish this.'

The man from the Town Hall waited, as the shopkeeper emptied the last of the bags. Then, just as he was about to emerge from behind the counter, a determined-looking woman plonked a large packet of washing powder in front of him.

'How much, Mr Reynolds?'

'One ninety-four.'

'It's not marked,' she said accusingly.

'Really? It should be. Under here somewhere.' He turned the packet upside down. 'Yes, there you are, see? One ninety-four.'

'You'd think they'd mark things where people could see,' said the customer, darkly.

'You would, madam, you would. There we are, then. Six pence change. Thank you.'

The woman scooped up her purchase, stared at Bradman with evident disapproval, and swept out.

'Sorry about that. Now, what can I do for you?'

The shopkeeper looked at him with polite enquiry.

'It's rather confidential,' Bradman replied.

'Could we go out in the back, somewhere?'

'Confidential? Oh well, I suppose so. Won't take long, will it? I've only got one staff on today.'

'Not long.'

He followed the tall figure through a door at the rear, and found himself in a small room which served as office and rest-room. There were three chairs on view.

'Would you mind if we sat down, Mr Reynolds?'

'Mind? No—er no—I suppose not.'

Reynolds sat next to a battered table, resting his elbow on it. He watched as the visitor seated himself, then asked quietly,

'Who are you really?'

Bradman was taken by surprise.

'You don't think I'm from the Town Hall?'

Reynolds shook his head decisively.

'Not in that suit,' he rejected. 'I know cloth, you see. Was in the tailoring once, myself.'

'Ah yes, of course,' comprehended Bradman. 'I was forgetting.'

There was a different expression on the grocer's face when he next spoke.

'Well then, if you know that, you must know quite a lot of things. I wasn't called Reynolds when I was in the tailoring. Changed my name since then. Well?'

Bradman had a distinct feeling that the initiative was slipping away from him, which wouldn't do at all.

'You are quite right, of course, I am not from the Town Hall. I only said that in order not to make your customers curious. I want to talk about your daughter, Maude Ryan.'

The older man nodded slowly, and there was a sudden slump to his shoulders.

'Yes,' he acknowledged quietly. 'I've been wondering how long it would be. She's dead you know. And the boy. Both of them. Car crash. Nearly two years ago, now. Still, I expect you know all that.'

'I have the background, yes. I'm very sorry, Mr—Reynolds. They were all the family you had, weren't they?'

Reynolds gave no sign of having heard.

'Lovely boy, he was. Bright as a button. She brought him up a treat, my Maude. Could have been married, you know, more than once, but she wouldn't have it. 'I can't afford to have my attention divided,' she used to say. That's what she used to say. 'Michael is going right to the top, and I'm going to spend my life getting him there.' I can hear her now. She'd have done it, too. Make no mistake about that. All such a waste. Everything. Just a waste. What happens now, then? Am I under arrest, or what?'

The tired eyes looked across, and Bradman realised, with a shock, that the speaker simply did not give a damn. It was all very disconcerting, the quiet unforced way in which the country grocer was leading the conversation. Bradman had expected a very different interview.

'You must have half-expected that someone like me would turn up in the end,' he said.

The response to this was the production of a packet of cigarettes.

'Do you smoke? It's all right, there's no food in here.'

After a brief hesitation, Bradman leaned forward and took one of the proffered tubes. Then he produced his lighter and pushed the little button at the side.

Reynolds chuckled.

'Savile Row suit and a gold lighter,' he observed. 'Don't know what the Town Hall union would say. Aren't you going to tell me who you are? You're no ordinary policeman, that's certain.'

'I'm what you might call an official public relations man,' was the reply. 'When someone prominent like Sir Francis Waterman dies, someone like me turns up, just to clear up any points that could cause embarrassment in high places.'

Reynolds nodded, as though he had been expecting something of the kind.

'Wondered if that might be it. Took you a while to get to me, though. I would have thought somebody would have turned up long before this.'

'Because the curry had to come from this shop, you mean?'

'Exactly. Mrs Cooper never shops anywhere else. There isn't anywhere else, not unless you take the bus into Guildford, and she hates crowds.'

Bradman flicked ash into an upturned tin lid.

'Didn't it occur to you that Mrs Cooper might have to take the blame?'

Reynolds was affronted.

'Certainly not. You don't imagine I'd have let them do that, do you? Nice woman like Mrs Cooper? I'd have come forward quick sharp, you may be sure.'

'Then how did you expect to get away with it? A couple of quick shots through a window would have been much more difficult to trace, and there could have been no suspicion of the housekeeper.'

Reynolds reached over awkwardly to deposit ash in the lid.

'Let me explain how I thought this out,' he suggested. 'Once I made up my mind to do it, that is. You're quite right about shooting him. That would have been more direct. Or a knife. Thought about that, too. The problem with any of those things was that the police would be in no doubt that it was murder. You can't cover up gunshots, and stab wounds and the like. You could never keep Mrs Cooper quiet, for one thing. Nor other people. Mortuary attendants, undertakers, all kinds of people. No, what I wanted was a method whereby

Waterman would die, but there would be a chance for the officials to have a breather. An opportunity to consider whether it suited their book to have the facts come out.'

He paused, waiting for some reaction.

'Are you suggesting you thought the authorities might decide to hush up an act of murder? That you might be allowed to get away with it?'

Reynolds shrugged.

'It's been known,' he said flatly. 'Waterman was a prominent man, and people at the top always have to make a quick survey of such a man's activities, decide how best to deal with the public. I was four years in an Intelligence unit, which I expect you also know. I haven't got much to learn about suppressing evidence, and making misleading reports. Greatest good of the greatest number, that's the rule. The higher up you go, the bigger the cover. It was worth a try. Anyway, you're here, aren't you?'

There was something in his tone that robbed the words of their most obvious meaning.

'What exactly do you mean by that?' queried Bradman.

'I mean, you are who you are, whatever that may be. There's no blue car outside. No police inspector telling me that anything I say, dah-de-dah. Just you. So I wasn't altogether wrong, was I? Something is on.'

There was a calmness about the man which

Bradman found most unsettling. A conversational approach which would have been more appropriate to a discussion on fly-fishing or something.

'Just think of me as an outrider, Mr Reynolds,' he advised. 'The main procession won't be far behind. Tell me something. Why did you kill Sir Francis Waterman?'

The man at the table elevated his eyebrows.

'I would have thought that was perfectly obvious,' he exclaimed. 'He ruined my daughter's life, put a fatherless boy into the world. Now they're gone, but he's still here. Do you know, I even sent him a clipping of the newspaper report of the accident, and what did I get? A letter from some secretary, telling me that Sir Francis had been sorry to read of my sad loss. My sad loss. Not his. Nothing to do with him, the bastard. Why did I want to kill him? You must be joking. I'm all alone in the world now. They're all gone. I took this little place after it happened. Changed my name, to get away from the past. Then, a couple of months ago, when I heard he'd just moved into the neighbourhood, it brought everything back. A man alone in the world has nothing to do but think. And when he's like me, all he thinks is bad thoughts.'

'But the timing,' insisted Bradman. 'Your daughter and your grandson have been gone for two years. If you'd lost control then, and attacked Waterman, even killed him, I could have understood it. So could many a jury, I've no doubt.'

'Just? At a trial, you mean? I'm just an ordinary man, not one of your violent sort, at all. I thought about doing for him then, as I had when it all started. But we all think like that sometimes, don't we? We all think about murder at some time in our lives, but we never do anything about it. I don't know whether it's fear, or whether we have too much to lose, or what. But we only talk. We don't do anything.'

That was true enough, thought Bradman. If murder was done every time someone wished someone else was dead, the population would quickly be decimated. This man was different, though, despite his words. He had translated thoughts into deeds.

'What you say is true, Mr Reynolds, but it doesn't alter the facts. You did kill him, didn't you?'

Reynolds scratched at his chin, half-smiling.

'You mentioned juries a minute ago. Well, I've already had my trial, Mr Bradman. Verdict, sentence and all. My heart's no good. There might be another six months in me, twelve at the outside. I could go tomorrow. I've even been to Harley Street. Top specialists. There's nothing to be done. That was what decided me, finally. I've nothing to lose, you see. Nothing. Not even my life. It's already spoken for.'

That would have to be checked, of course,

and Bradman would see to that. But he knew it would be no more than a formality. There was no mistaking the quiet acceptance on the face of this man.

'I see,' he replied slowly. 'Would you have any objection if a reference was made to your doctor?'

'Refer away,' was the rejoinder. 'I only wish he could tell you something different. Well, what are you going to do?'

Bradman stared into the middle distance for a long minute before replying.

'Haven't quite made up my mind,' he admitted. 'A lot depends on whether you're to be trusted, Mr Reynolds.'

'How do you mean? Trusted not to kill anybody else? You needn't worry about that.'

The visitor shook his head.

'No, I don't mean that. Let's just suppose for a moment that I could arrange to forget this conversation. How am I to know that you haven't written everything down somewhere, so that it can be published after your death? We're only supposing, mind.'

Reynolds looked horrified.

'You haven't thought that through, have you? You haven't thought what it would mean. An article like that might damage Waterman's reputation, if anyone would look at it. But think about my dead girl, my grandson. You think I could go to my grave, knowing that their names would be dragged through the mud? Come on, Mr Bradman. Have another think.'

It was the most animation he had shown since the conversation began, and the listener was left in no doubt as to his sincerity. Bradman was satisfied.

He stood up, and the man opposite did likewise. They looked at each other carefully.

'I don't think it would be in the best interests of all concerned for this to go any further,' said Bradman, staring straight into his listener's eyes. 'There's nothing anyone can do to bring back the dead, and I don't think the living would profit very much if all this became public knowledge. No guarantees, mark you, but I shall be surprised if you hear any more about this.'

Reynolds nodded, but said nothing. His face was ineffably sad.

Bradman left him standing there, and walked out through the shop. There was a public telephone-box outside the neighbouring post office. He went inside and dialled Aunt Alice.

After identifying himself, he said, 'Tell Auntie I've finished wrapping that parcel. I'm ready for some new supplies, when available.'

He walked back to the car, and started the engine.

Have to watch the signs this time, if he didn't want to finish up back in Guildford.